The Seventh Armada Ghost Book

This Armada book belongs to:

_____

_____

_____

Also in Armada

The Seventh Armada Ghost Book

Edited by Mary Danby

Illustrated by Peter Archer

The Seventh Armada Ghost Book was first
published in the U.K. in 1975 by
William Collins Sons & Co. Ltd.,
14 St. James's Place, London S.W.1.

The arrangement of this collection is copyright
© Mary Danby 1975.

Printed in Great Britain by Love & Malcomson Ltd.,
Brighton Road, Redhill, Surrey.

CONTENTS

ACKNOWLEDGEMENTS

The editor gratefully acknowledges permission to reprint copyright material to the following:

Joyce Marsh for THE SHEPHERD'S DOG (© Joyce Marsh 1975)

Pamela Vincent for WHEN THE MOON WAS FULL (© Pamela Vincent 1975)

Julia Birley for THE LIFE AND SOUL OF THE PARTY (© Julia Birley 1975)

Brian Morse for A CAT ON THE DRIVE (© Brian Morse 1975)

Lucy Norris for PORTRAIT OF RHODA (© Lucy Norris 1975)

Kay Leith for THE TOCKLEY FAMILIAR (© Kay Leith 1975)

Sydney J. Bounds for THE HANGING TREE (© Sydney J. Bounds 1975)

Mary Clarke for THE OLD MAN OF THE HILLS (© Mary Clarke 1975)

RAY GOTTLEIB for THE FUN FAIR GHOST (© Ray Gottleib 1975)

Tim Vicary for THE CURSE OF THE WHITE OWL (© Tim Vicary 1975)

Rosemary Timperley for THE MAN WITH THE BEARD (© Rosemary Timperley 1975)

THE HAUNTERS is © Mary Danby 1975

Introduction

Do you read ghost stories in bed? Does the light throw strange shadows on the walls? Do you wonder what might come out of the wardrobe? It's all part of the fun, of course —the fun of frightening yourself.

But be careful. Some of the stories in this book could give you colder shivers than you'd bargained for. So I recommend that it should be read in strong sunlight by all but the *very* bravest.

The Shepherd's Dog is a marvellous story of a sheepdog left alone when his Master dies—and it's haunting in more than one sense. Read it and you'll see what I mean.

Have you ever wandered off along a beach and thought you couldn't find your way back? This is what happens in *When the Moon Was Full*, a tale of a strange and mystical night on the north-west coast of Australia.

The Life and Soul of the Party is the jovial, capering conjurer. But his disappearing trick is a little too real for some . . . And there's another vanishing act in *A Cat on the Drive*. Michael tries to stroke the cat—but his hand encounters nothing at all!

In *Portrait of Rhoda*, terror intrudes on a midnight feast as a girl relives her vengeful past, while in *The Tockley Familiar*, Derek faces a spectacle so horrific that it could only come from the very depths of Hell.

For ghost addicts who like Westerns, *The Hanging Tree* combines both. It's a vivid tale of an episode at Tombstone Gulch. One can almost hear the jangling spurs! And from the mysterious East comes *The Old Man of the Hills*, complete with a long, wispy beard—and a pigtail.

7

A ghost can be quite useful in the right circumstances. *The Fun Fair Ghost* certainly is—even if his conversation is a few hundred years out of date. "Sirrahs" and "Avaunts" are all very well, but what really counts is whether or not he can tickle!

Some say that white owls are the lost souls of the dead. Are they? In *The Curse of the White Owl*, their shrieks seem to be almost human—despairing cries for release from a nightmare punishment. And on the subject of nightmares, don't read *The Man with the Beard* unless you like your stories gruesome. It's a real blood-curdler.

A lot of people would like to see a ghost—"a real dead one", as Jack says in *The Haunters*. But ghost-hunting can be a dangerous pursuit—especially if you try to haunt the haunters!

A dozen supernatural tales—for your shuddering enjoyment.

MARY DANBY

THE SHEPHERD'S DOG

by JOYCE MARSH

CHAUVAL lifted his head sharply; his sensitive, upstanding ears twitched as he listened intently. From outside the window a little twig scraped against the pane and the big white dog recognised it as the sound which had roused him from his uneasy sleep. His body relaxed as he allowed his shaggy head to drop down on to his forepaws.

He did not sleep again, however, as his olive-green eyes, lightly flecked with little pin-points of golden light, stared fixedly at the still form on the bed. For two long days he had watched that figure, waiting to see the tiniest movement of life, although by now his every sense told him that he hoped in vain.

On the first morning when the Master had not risen as he usually did at first light of day, Chauval had been impatient and slightly irritable. Even through the closed window his sensitive nose had picked up the exhilarating scent of the new day. His limbs had almost ached in their eagerness for that glorious, rushing scamper over the heather which began his every morning.

Restlessly he had padded around the room, scratched at the closed door and lifted his head to savour the fresh, clean smell of a new day. Then a long deep growl had begun low in his throat, but still the Master had not moved. The growl had become a whine, anxiety replaced impatience and Chauval had crept closer to the bed. He had thrust his nose beneath the Master's shoulder and nudged him violently. The man's head rolled on the pillow, but he had not opened his eyes nor made a sound. One still hand dangled from the bed; Chauval licked it—it was so cold.

Then the big, shaggy white dog had jumped on to the bed, covering the man with his body, licking at his face and hands as he tried to drive out that dreadful cold with the warmth of his own body.

It was then that the vague anxiety had become a sickening fear, for the Master's well-known scent had gone and in its place was a smell that Chauval knew and dreaded.

So many times in his long working life the sheepdog had found a sheep which had wandered too near the edge and had fallen to its death on the rocky beach below, or a straying lamb which had become stranded on a ledge to die of fear and hunger. All these animals had the smell of death on them, and now that same hateful scent was upon the Master.

Chauval, in his panic, had leapt from the bed and rushed first to the door and then to the window, his head lifted in a long, despairing wail. Instinctively he knew that with his great strength and size he could, if he chose, break out of the room, but without direct orders from the Master, he dared not try.

All his life, ever since he had first come as a tiny puppy to the lonely cliff-top cottage, the Master had ordered and directed his every action. It was the Master who had taught him how to guard sheep, it was he who had told the dog what to do and when to do it. Even in those carefree, happy moments when work was done and the shepherd's dog was at liberty to rush pell-mell over the springy turf and wind-scorched heather, Chauval never forgot the law of instant obedience, for his playtime began on the Master's command and ended with his whistling call.

Chauval had been happy and secure in his trusting devotion, but now the Master's voice was still and the dog was alone and desolate. In his bewilderment and confusion there was only one thing of which he could be certain. When he was alone his duty was to stay on guard, so for two long days and nights he had been in his room. Even the gnawing hunger and thirst were forgotten as he crouched low, every muscle of his body tense and alert to protect his Master and his home.

Suddenly Chauval's head lifted again as another, much louder noise came from outside and the draught, blowing in through a broken pane, carried the scent of a human. Silently, but with his lip lifted in the beginnings of a snarl, Chauval moved to the window and raised himself on hind legs to look out.

On the path, a few yards from the cottage, stood a man. His head was thrown back as he shouted loudly:

"Are ye in there, Will? Are ye all right then, Will?"

Chauval looked back quickly towards the bed, half hoping that the sound of a voice might have called the Master back to life; but still there was no movement from the bed.

The dark-haired man, still calling the Master's name, had come very close to the cottage and was rapping on the door with his heavy stick. Chauval's snarl became more menacing and the hairs on his back stood up stiffly. He knew that man and he knew that stick. Once, a very long time ago, he had felt its weight upon his back; the man had come into the cottage whilst Chauval was alone and had walked into rooms and looked into places where only the Master was allowed to go. The dog had barked once in warning and the man had hit him with the stick. Now that man was an enemy—never to be allowed inside.

The knocking on the door had ceased as the man walked around the cottage, looking in at all the windows. He came to Chauval's window and stopped to peer inside. For a brief moment the man and the dog stared into each

11

other's eyes. The sound of the dog's angry barking echoed in the room and the man leapt back in startled fear.

But he realised that he was protected by the glass between them and he came forward again to look past the frantic dog into the room. He stared in for a moment and then, turning quickly, he ran off. Chauval fell silent. In the distance he could hear the soft, melancholy bleating of the sheep and, further away still, the wild rushing of the sea hurling itself against the barren, rocky beach.

Stiffly he dropped down from the window and crept back to resume his vigil by the bed, but, weakened by lack of food and little sleep, the spate of barking had exhausted him and his eyes closed again in slumber.

A long time must have passed, for the room was almost dark when Chauval was once more roused by the sound of footsteps and loud voices.

There was a violent banging on the cottage door and Chauval heard it fly open with a crash. Swiftly, he leapt on to the bed, crouching over the defenceless Master. He was sweating with fear and the perspiration ran off his tongue to hang in wet, sticky streams from his mouth.

The voices came nearer and nearer; the bedroom door flew open and in the opening was the Man with the Stick. The huge white dog remained motionless, hunched protectively and tense above his Master's body. His lip curled upward, showing long, yellow teeth, and the whites of his eyes gleamed through the dusk.

"The great ugly brute will ne'er let us come near. We'll have to shoot him first."

It was that harsh rough voice of the Man with the Stick. Chauval gathered himself to spring, but suddenly someone else spoke, softly and gently.

"Poor thing, he must have been locked in here for days. He's half starved. Maybe I can coax him out."

The cruel voice muttered and mumbled, but the man

stood aside and his place in the doorway was taken by a stranger.

"Good dog, come on then, we'll not hurt you, good boy, that's a good dog."

The stranger's voice was kind and reassuring. He held out the back of his hand with the fingers hanging limply down.

"Good dog, come here then."

With infinite slowness, Chauval eased himself off the bed. Never taking his eyes from the stranger's face, the dog crawled slowly across the floor. With all his heart he wanted to trust this man.

"For heaven's sake get on wi' it. We haven't got all night to mess around wi' yon vicious brute."

The harsh voice spat out the words, and out of the corner of his eye Chauval saw the stick raised above him. With a powerful spring he leapt up, and his teeth fastened in the hand holding the stick. He felt the warm taste of blood in his mouth as his body thudded into the man's chest and bore him backwards to the floor.

The room was full of noise and the smell of human fear. The stranger's voice, no longer gentle, was raised above the others and his was the hand which snatched up the stick and brought it down hard on the dog's back. With a yelp of pain and anger, Chauval turned to snarl a brief defiance at the stranger who was now another enemy and then he sprang past the men towards the open door. Frantic hands grabbed at his long fur but, snapping and snarling, the dog pulled himself free and leapt outside. With a few bounding strides he reached the cover of the bushes and threw himself down in the tangled bracken.

In an agony of confusion and fear he stared at the cottage. He wanted to go back inside to continue his guard over the Master, but he dared not. Lights had sprung up in the windows and the sound of voices drifted out. The front door stood open and suddenly two men came out carrying something wrapped in white. Instinctively, Chauval knew that it was the Master.

The Man with the Stick had brought the strangers and Chauval had been driven out. They had forced him to abandon his post, and now his enemies were taking the Master away. The big dog raised himself up on to his haunches, his green eyes glittered in the twilight darkness and he began to whimper softly. Then he flung back his head, the long snout pointing directly upwards towards the pale moon, and the whimper became a long howl of desolation and despair.

"There he is, over there! Shoot him, someone, while ye've got the chance. He'll be no good now old Will's gone and if he turns rogue he'll be a menace to all of us."

It was the harsh, cruel voice, and close upon the words came a sharp crack and a singing bullet passed close to the dog's ear.

Chauval began to run as he had never run in his life before. Leaping, bounding, with lolling tongue and eyes bulging until they were nearly bursting from the sockets, he crashed through the bracken and undergrowth.

The lights in the cottage receded to pin points and the shouts of the men were borne away on the night breeze, and still Chauval ran. The scrubby trees and bushes thinned and the ground beneath his feet became more sharp and rocky as he fled up the steep, craggy hill which rose sharply from the cliff-top pasture. At last he could run no more and he flung himself down on to a flat rock.

His sides heaved and the breath rasped in his throat. The pounding of his heart quietened at last and he breathed more easily, but now he was tormented by thirst.

The big dog raised his head and the sensitive nostrils quivered as he explored the night wind for the longed-for scent of water. His senses told him that water was not far

14

away, but he did not immediately go to find it. Instead he peered anxiously down the slope and listened intently. In his headlong flight he had taken no care to hide his trail and his enemies could easily track him down.

To his relief he could hear only the sound of rushing wind; for the moment he was safe. Gleaming wraith-like in the darkness, the dog weaved a cautious zig-zagging course towards the water. The clear mountain stream flowed abundantly. Bursting out from a fissure in the rock, it cascaded first into a deep pool before it ran off down the hillside. Chauval thrust his muzzle into the icy water and greedily drank his fill.

He was ravenously hungry, but the wild, rushing escape up the steep hill had drained the last of his strength and he was too exhausted to search for food. A flat, jutting shelf of rock offered him some shelter and he crept beneath it. Wearily he buried his nose into the long warm hairs on his flank and slept.

Chauval awoke at the first light of day and his first thought was the gnawing, agonising hunger. He had never in his life needed to find his own food; no one had ever taught him how and now he had no idea where to begin. He whimpered and whined, calling for the Master. Even now he could still desperately hope to hear a whistle or the beloved voice calling his name, but all was silent except for the tinkling water and the lonely singing of the wind.

His green eyes flicked restlessly as he surveyed the barren hillside—there was no food here. There would be food in the cottage if only he dared go to find it. Hunger overcame fear at last and, moving carefully, with his body close to the ground, he crept down the hill.

The cottage was deserted: the strangers had gone and the Master had not returned. In the pale light of dawn the dog moved around the house, scratching at the closed doors, but there was no way to get in. The sheep, left unguarded, had strayed into the tangled undergrowth near the cottage, where they bleated dismally. Instinctively Chauval moved around them, expertly gathering them into a little flock and herding them back to the grazing land. Enviously he watched them eat their fill of the succulent grass.

Suddenly he heard the sound of a single sheep in distress and behind a large rock he found a young ewe with her lamb stretched out on the ground beside her. It had fallen from the top of the rock and its fleece was streaked with blood. The mother bleated pathetically, but the lamb was quite dead. With an expert little rush, Chauval drove the ewe away and nudged the lamb with his nose. It was still warm and the sickly sweet smell of the fresh blood made the juices flow in his mouth; but it was forbidden to eat the flesh of a dead sheep and Chauval would not disobey the Master's law—he would die first.

"Good dog, you may eat the lamb."

The well-known voice sounded loud and clear in his ear. With a little yelp of joyful surprise, Chauval looked round. The breeze blew in off the sea and the sheep called softly to each other, but there was neither scent nor sight of the Master. Yet his voice came again, urgently.

"Eat, Chauval—eat or you will die."

The pangs of desperate hunger gnawed agonisingly at his insides, but there was no need now to hesitate. Somehow and from somewhere far off the Master had spoken.

The long yellow teeth ripped and tore at the soft flesh as, with ravenous haste, the dog wolfed down the fresh meat. So intent was he upon satisfying his hunger that he did not immediately notice that he was no longer alone on the cliff top. A man, a woman and a boy were running towards him. They were shouting and waving their arms

16

when Chauval heard them at last and looked up from his meal. He gave a quick, welcoming bark, for he knew them and they were his friends. Suddenly the youth bent down and picked something up from the ground. The next moment a sharp, hard rock flew through the air to hit the dog a stinging blow on the head. He yelped in pain and surprise; there was no doubting now the menace in their voices and gestures. Suddenly and inexplicably even these friends had become his enemies. Once more he fled upwards to safety. The full and satisfying meal had restored his strength and he moved swiftly.

The people stood by the bloody remnants of the lamb and watched him go.

"That were Will's old dog," the boy said.

"Aye an' I should've had my gun handy. He'll have to be shot now—he's turned sheep killer."

The woman answered her husband and there was pity in her voice. "Poor thing. 'Twill be a mercy to put him down or like as not he'll starve to death, for he'll not let us near him, that's for sure."

And so the barren rocky hill became Chauval's home and refuge. Water he had in abundance, but food was a constant, nagging problem. Once or twice he had managed to catch a young rabbit, but mostly he lived by what he could scrounge or steal from the scattered cottages on the cliff top. He had always to take care to search for his food when the people were asleep, for at the very sight of him they drove him off with sticks and stones and guns.

At night or in the light of early dawn he slunk down the hill, moving cautiously with his body close to the ground. The Master's voice had never come again to give him leave, so he would not touch the sheep. In the pale light he moved like a great white shadow through the flock, and they, knowing him to be their friend, never ceased their constant nibbling at the grass as he passed.

17

While the cottagers slept, he padded silently around their homes, sniffing and searching for the scraps they had thrown away. Sometimes he ate the foul-smelling mash which the good wives had put out for their chickens. At other times he found a clutch of eggs laid in the undergrowth by a straying hen. Once in his maraudings he was attacked by a little half-wild cat; he had killed it and in his desperation had eaten even that.

In the weeks since the Master had gone the sheepdog had grown thin and gaunt. His long coat, wetted by the rain and dried by the sun and salt breezes, was filthy and matted. Twigs, thorns and brambles had become tangled in the long hairs, where they fretted and scratched his skin when he lay down.

At night, especially when the moon rode high in the heavens, he yearned so desperately for the Master that he lifted his snout to the stars and let forth a long, desolate howl. Below, in the little hamlet, the people would hear his mournful wail and shudder in their warm, cosy beds.

One morning he had been particularly unsuccessful in his search for food; the sun had risen and the cottagers were stirring, yet his ravenous hunger would not allow him to abandon his scavenging. Suddenly he heard a door opening nearby and, in a quick, panicky scamper, he made for a clump of bracken, where he pressed his body close to the ground and trembled.

The cheerful sound of a woman's voice drifted out through the open door, and a few minutes later a tiny child, tottering on unsteady legs, came out into the garden. Chauval pressed down even further into the concealing bracken and his heart thudded painfully. The little boy was coming closer and the dog dared not move, for he could not escape without being seen.

With the casual curiosity of the very young, the child was peering into the bushes. Suddenly he saw the white

18

dog and his eyes opened wide in surprise. For a moment he swayed uncertainly on chubby little legs and then plumped down in front of Chauval.

"Hello, doggy," he lisped. "Do you want thum buppy?"

With trusting friendliness he offered a thick crust of bread liberally spread with butter. Chauval took the food gently in his front teeth and wolfed it down. The boy gurgled his pleasure and stretched out his little hand to scratch and tickle at the sensitive spot behind the dog's ears. It was so long since Chauval had felt a loving, friendly touch. His delight in it now made him forget even his hunger. He crept forward and rested his head on the child's lap.

"Does doggy want thum more buppy?"

The little boy scrambled clumsily to his feet.

"Come on, doggy, let's get more buppy."

He set off towards his home, encouraging his new friend to follow. Longing to feel again that loving, friendly touch, Chauval crawled out of his hiding place. With tail tucked between his legs and head hanging low he slunk after the boy, but his progress was slow and the child grew impatient.

"Come on, silly doggy."

He grasped the dog's ears in both his little hands and tugged with all his strength. In an excess of grateful affection Chauval reached up and licked the baby's face, and it was at that moment that a piercing shriek rang out from the cottage doorway. A woman's voice shouted urgently:

"Husband, come quickly! The killer dog's got our Ian!"

Chauval leapt sideways and the child, startled by the note of fear in his mother's voice, ran to hide himself in her skirts. The woman was thrust aside and her place in the doorway was taken by a man. It was the Man with the Stick, only now it was not a stick but a gun that he held in his hand.

The terrified dog raced for the concealing cover of the undergrowth, but he was too late. The shot sounded almost in his ear and the searing bullet ran along his side, gouging a deep, bloody weal in its path.

For a moment or two Chauval ran on and felt no pain, but after a while his limbs stiffened and every thudding step was agony to him. He knew he could never reach the safety of his rocky retreat and he veered off towards the only other hiding place he knew—the tall rock on the cliff, behind which he had found and eaten the lamb.

He reached the rock and crept gratefully into its concealing shadow, pressing himself as close as he could to the cool, rough rock.

The bullet wound was painful, and for a long while he diligently licked at it until his rough tongue had cleaned it and soothed the pain. Weakened by the lack of food, and exhausted by the effort, he fell into a deep sleep.

When he awoke, the sun had long since reached its peak and had begun on its slow slide down towards the sea. Chauval was thirsty, his nose felt hot and dry and the inside of his mouth burned feverishly. He longed for the cool waters of his mountain stream and he peered cautiously out of his hiding place. The sound of human voices drifted over to him and the dog drew back in alarm.

Not far away, across the rich green pasture, a man, a woman and several children were playing with a ball. They laughed and shouted in their play, but their gaiety brought neither comfort nor reassurance to Chauval. He knew that he had but to show himself and their happy voices would become rough and harsh as they came at him with their sticks and their guns.

Behind him the cliff dropped down sheer to the sea. There was no escape that way and the only way to safety was barred by the group on the cliff-top.

Patiently the big, white dog settled down to await his opportunity to slip past his enemies. As he watched, one of the children wandered away from the group and, unnoticed by the others, came towards Chauval and the cliff edge.

The breeze carried his scent to the dog's sensitive nose and he recognised the tiny boy who had befriended him that morning. The child tottered to the very edge and, with all the strength in his fat little arms, threw a pebble out over the cliff. He chuckled as it rattled and clattered on to the beach below.

So many times Chauval had seen the Master's sheep venture too near to the crumbling edge of the cliff, and he knew what should be done. Like the sheep, this human child should be herded back to safety. Yet, if he were to venture out, he would be seen and the man would attack.

The boy swayed dangerously on the very edge and Chauval could not decide what he must do. In his anxiety he whimpered softly.

As he watched the child with an ever-increasing confusion there came upon him an icy chill and he began to tremble violently. A small misty cloud had drifted in from the sea, enveloping him in its clammy touch. The hairs on his neck bristled and then, from somewhere in the vapour which hung over him, came the voice he had so longed to hear.

"Chauval, my good Chauval," it called. "Go then boy, fetch him back."

There was no hesitation now. The Master had spoken and Chauval leapt to obey.

"Steady boy, easy now," the voice called from behind, and the good sheepdog lay down in the grass. Then, quietly, so as not to startle the child, he moved forward in a series of little rushes. As soon as he was able, the dog placed himself between the boy and the cliff edge. The child, unafraid, lunged towards him, gurgling his pleasure, but with a warning snarl Chauval forced him back. Again the child came on, and this time the dog herded him away from the edge with a little nip on the fatty part of his leg. More startled than hurt, the boy gave a loud indignant wail and ran at his protector with his clenched fists—but again Chauval urged him backwards from the cliffs.

The man and the woman had heard their son's cry and were hurrying to his rescue. Chauval paid them no heed as, with all the skill he had learned from guarding sheep, he forced the child to safety. It was the man who reached the child first and snatched him up in his arms.

"Get away, you evil brute."

He lashed out with his heavy boot. Chauval leapt back, but the blow caught him full in the chest, forcing him nearer to the edge. The man aimed yet another vicious kick and the dog felt his back legs slip away into space. The weight of his body dragged down and he clawed frantically at the soft turf with his front feet. For a brief moment he hung suspended, but his grip was too tenuous and he fell.

Tumbling and twisting, Chauval hurtled down. The sea-gulls got up from their rocky perches and their shrieks mingled with the screams of the doomed dog. His body smashed down on to the rocks and earth; sea and sky were blotted out in one final stab of pain.

The blood-streaked flanks heaved once, twice, and were still. The birds settled back on the rocky ledges and, from above, the man and the woman looked down on the still shape so far below them.

22

"Well, that's the last trouble we'll get from that vicious dog," the man said with cruel satisfaction.

"Aye," said his wife, "an' it might have been our Ian lyin' doon there. We've only the dog to thank that it isn't."

The man looked askance.

"You're a fool, husband," she went on. "You've seen a dog work sheep often enough. Could ye no see that it weren't attacking our boy? He were herdin' him back from the edge—just like he would sheep."

The man hung his head. "Well, he's gone wild. He's better off this way, anyhow," he said sulkily.

"Aye," she said, and they moved off, while the child in his father's arms whined, "Nice doggy, where's 'at nice doggy gone?"

All was now very quiet upon the beach. The sun had dipped its rim into the sea and the shadows grew long and dark. A shrill whistle sounded in the breeze and a dark mist at the water's edge trembled like the heat haze of high summer. The misty cloud steadied and darkened and took shape. The whistle came again and a soft, white vapour hung over the body of the dead dog.

The cloud by the water's edge took on the shape of a man and he stretched forth his hand.

"Chauval."

The name was a soft sigh on the sea breeze. A great shaggy dog bounded forward, leaving behind the dead, blood-stained thing on the rocks.

The man moved off over the sands and the dog by his side leapt and danced in a transport of delight.

Few people now will venture down on to that part of the beach, for it is said that, in the late afternoon, just as the sun is about to slide into the sea, a man and his dog walk the sands. Those who have seen them say that the dog's olive-green eyes forever glow with a loving devotion, while the man smiles his contentment, and, as they pass, the air turns cold and is filled with soft sounds. Even the little waves breaking on the shore sing out the name . . . "Chauval, Chauval . . ."

WHEN THE MOON WAS FULL

by PAMELA VINCENT

THE moon was full and very bright that evening, golden and so big that it seemed menacing, much too close to earth. Not a good moon for fishing by any means, but the tide was right and Dad was restless, so we went anyway.

Besides, the fish around Australia's northwest coast make their own rules, and we'd caught them often enough before at the wrong time—or with the wrong bait on the wrong hook for that matter! We didn't really mind whether we caught anything or not; it's peaceful along those empty shores with no sound but the everlasting saraband of the surf, and not another soul within miles. Night falls early in the tropics and sometimes we spend hours there by the sea, watching a million million diamonds parading slowly across the whole black velvet sky.

"Why don't you scout round for some wood to make a fire?" Dad suggested. "The wind's coming up cool now."

There are always plenty of dead branches and odd planks or bits of timber lying about, as well as the litter that pollutes even the loneliest spots, so I floundered through deep, soft sand and scrambled on my knees up the dunes that led to bushland dividing us from the track where we had left our long-suffering old car.

24

It was early, the huge moon still low in the sky, and I was climbing straight into its glowing disc. The light stretched out towards me like something alive, greedy, trying to draw me into itself.

"What do you want of me?" I called, foolishly.

With an effort, I dragged my eyes away and hunched my shoulders to break the spell before I lost my senses to that hungry moon.

"Moon madness, what next?" I chided myself.

I tried to put my mind to the job in hand, but that silvery glow was all around me in a gossamer embrace that smothered my will-power. I wanted only to get away, to hurry back to Dad and safety.

Safety from *what*? What ever could happen to me in moonlight as bright as day? I didn't know, I just felt danger in the air.

There was no wood that I could see. We'd have to make do with dead branches and armfuls of dried-up bush, but that should be enough for a little while—it didn't feel so cold now. The wind had dropped after all and everything was very still, the bare landscape eerie in that strange light.

I quickly gathered up as much brushwood as I could carry and, glancing over my shoulder, picked my way back, staggering across the rough ground. I thought I knew where I was going, but when I came in sight of the sea there was no sign of Dad—not even his fishing-rod stuck in a cleft in the rocks. I looked for a clue from my footprints but the sand was smooth in front of me, smooth and clean and untouched-looking.

It couldn't be far, but which way?

"Dad?"

The silence threw my voice back at me, but there was no answer. Muttering darkly, I flung down my bundle of firewood. I'd have to find Dad first and come back for it.

25

Only I didn't find him! I *knew* I couldn't have gone far in the short time I'd been away, and neither could Dad, carrying all our gear, yet the fact remained that he just wasn't there.

Calling out from time to time, I searched to see whether he had climbed down to the water's edge, hidden by a rocky outcrop, but he'd disappeared as if the ground—or the sea?—had swallowed him up. I began to feel scared, imagining him slipping on a loose stone, falling and striking his head, being snatched out to sea by one of those waves that suddenly dart inland ahead of the tide in a surge of surf.

But our fishing-bag and ice-box would still be there, I told myself firmly. I could have sworn that I was standing on the flat patch of rock where we'd left them. I seemed to recognize the shape of the rocks around me: there was one like a little tombstone, for instance, sticking up-right next to a pool of water left by the last high tide.

I went back to where I had left the firewood and turned to stare seawards again. The brightest stars, competing with the moonglow, made a familiar pattern. I had to be in the right place, and yet—and yet I could see only one set of footprints, the ones I had just made.

I remembered that when we'd arrived there had been someone's bare feet and a dog's paws, a motor-bike's tyre track. Here you would never know that anyone had ever passed this way. Even the empty cans and bottles and bits of wrappings were missing. Everything looked unreal, frozen.

"Dad! Dad!"

I called and called. He must hear me! There was no wind to carry my voice away and the pounding of the surf was gentle.

There was nothing for it but to make my way back to the car and wait until Dad noticed my absence and came looking for me—which might be hours. I've never known anyone lose himself like Dad in his own world of fishing. But he'd never been as lost as this, and if he meant to tease me he wouldn't let the joke go stale like this.

I couldn't find the car! I couldn't even find the track. There were my footprints amongst the sandy graveyard of shells where I'd been gathering up wood, but none leading out of it. The bush stretched away in the moonlight, flat and featureless, and although the road was somewhere beyond, I knew it twisted and turned like the many tracks leading to the shore, and I walked in circles without coming upon any of them.

"This is impossible, a nightmare," I told myself. *But I was awake.* "That stupid moon!"

It was higher in the sky now, smaller and whiter but casting just as much of its light to confuse me. I shouldn't be lost if it were *daylight*.

"I hate you, Moon!"

Slipping and sliding in the sand, I tried to run back to the sea. If I could only stay next to the water, follow the coastline, I'd have to end up at the jetty by the township. It might take me hours or days but I'd get there in the end. There was nothing else I could do.

I stood gasping on top of the dunes, my heart beating much too fast so that I could hardly breathe, and—oh, blessed relief! This time I saw Dad, sitting hunched up on the sand.

"Oh, Dad! Dad! Where have you been?"

I ran towards him, not worrying that I was falling more than walking, but he might have been a statue for all the notice he took. Really, these keen fishermen!

But where was his rod? And our bag and ice-box?

"Dad?" My voice was uncertain.

It was then I saw he was naked. It wasn't Dad at all!

I stopped, horror-struck.

Who was it? What was he doing here?

The man raised his head and stared towards me, or rather, he stared through me. I felt he didn't see me at all. He was an Aboriginal.

An Aboriginal *here*? There weren't any in this area, not even the westernized kind, certainly no tribesmen. Long ago they had made their cave-drawings throughout this remote cape, but now none was nearer than four or five hundred miles away—the wild men had vanished.

I was not mistaken. The moonlight was so bright that I could make out every feature, the weird tribal markings on face and body. Why didn't he see me, though? Was he blind? Or merely waiting for me to go away?

I turned, and caught a movement from the tail of my eye, quite close to me. Another Aboriginal——

I shrank back, but this one ignored me as much as the first. He stepped forward proudly, his bare feet disdaining the clinking sand that made me so clumsy, and I could see his eyes gleaming in the ebony face.

At once the seated man fell forward, grovelling in the sand. I was astonished. He was worshipping, as if in the presence of a god!

Then he went back to his hunched position, clasping bony knees with sticklike arms, and stayed as motionless as before.

The god, if such he was, silently and gracefully began to dance. Quietly at first, then growing louder, I became aware of the sound of chanting voices and—that must be the droning of a didgeridoo, the rattle of music sticks, a drum, a conch. All round me the air vibrated with this music that had never meant anything to me on a tape-recording but now filled me with awe of the unknown.

Perhaps to a man of the Stone Age there is nothing un-natural about one of his gods appearing before him, but I couldn't believe my eyes. I sank to the ground, knowing that I should not be there, should not be watching: females are not permitted to share the tribal ceremonies, and who knew what dreadful penalty I might have to pay for my intrusion? I shuddered but I couldn't tear myself away.

The weird music grew wilder, the dancing more frenzied and yet controlled; there was a pattern to it. Suddenly the seated man rose to his feet and started to follow the other's steps, copying every movement until, after a time, he was no longer following but was wrapped up within himself, continuing the dance after the god had ceased.

I watched the dancer and did not see the god depart, and soon the music faded away to leave us in a throbbing silence. The man's movements slowed, stopped, and he stood sunk in reverie for a long moment, then slowly he walked away from me along the shore. Rapt, I watched the slender figure until I could see it no more.

Only then did I realize that, in all that bright moonlight, neither of them had cast a shadow. And in all that deep sand, neither of them had left footprints.

Thoughtfully, I went back to where I had left the firewood, and stubbed my toe on a crumpled lemonade can. The marks of a dog's paws beside a tyre track stood out clearly.

"Hullo, what took you so long?"

Dad's voice was calm and he was really more interested in the tip of his rod, dipping gently, than in my reply. It wasn't the time to tell him what had happened to me, if I ever could tell anyone.

What had happened to me? Somehow the magic moon, no longer my enemy, had caused a cog in Time's wheel to slip and allow me to share a moment from the age of myths, when mankind learnt directly from the gods. The sacred dances of today's Aborigines recall that moment when their ancestor became the chosen vessel of the gods to hold their tribal secrets, and I had entered into the

29

Dreamtime—when the world was young—to see how it all began. Nothing would ever seem quite the same for me again.

"Thank you, Moon," I whispered, as she smiled down at me from the highest point in the sky. "I'm sorry I didn't trust you before."

It was a beautiful night, that night when the moon was full.

THE LIFE AND SOUL OF THE PARTY

by JULIA BIRLEY

DOWN in Penge where I live there used to be a huge dilapidated church, all pointed windows and grinning gargoyles. One day the surveyors came to look round and make plans to knock it down and build a new one. Mr. and Mrs. Cox, who lived close by, saw them out of their front window as they sat sorting prizes for the Parish Children's Party. They had quite an argument. Mr. Cox was attached to the old St. Ethelburga's. His wife decidedly was not.

"It's just a useless bit of run-down Victorian gothic. A regular rocky horror. People throw their litter into the graveyard. It gives me the creeps."

"But it's got character. It's got traditions," insisted Mr. Cox, who was romantic. "Those Victorians were a dynamic lot. They thought big. Look at the Crystal Palace——"

"How can I? It was burnt down."

"But can't you imagine it—all glittering? The fountains, the marbles—my word, if they could see what it looks like now!"

"It's enough to make them rise from their graves," Mrs.

30

Cox agreed. "And not only the buildings. Look at the way kids behave nowadays. I can tell you I'm dreading this party in the Church Hall. Wish we'd never got roped in for it.'

"We could certainly do with a spot of Victorian discipline. Especially when Larry Murdoch and that young Trevor get going. Now when St. Ethelburga's was first built, people had ways of dealing with infant greasers. They were seen and not heard."

"I dare say it will be all right," Mrs. Cox said. "So long as you manage to keep them running about."

Mr. Cox did not feel too sure of that, as he went over to the church next day about an hour before the kick-off. The Parish ladies had been busy, putting holly round the door and Chinese lanterns all along the dark south aisle, which led through to the lighted hall where the party was to be. But it would have taken more than that to cheer up St. Ethelburga's. The prim, tall pillars, the black vaults overhead and the smell of musty hymn books all seemed to say: How dare you? What is the meaning of this disgusting frivolity? Mr. Cox shivered slightly, and just then something butted him from behind. Several children, arrived much too early, went stampeding past to the hall, their innocent faces aglow as they barged against each other with gleeful yells. Mr. Cox went after them, feeling tired already.

Just inside the hall, he caught the two worst boys nicking sausage rolls from the buffet. "Understand," he said, grabbing Trevor by the collar. "I want no funny business from either of you this evening."

Trevor rolled his eyes and smirked. "I dunno what you mean." His mate Larry belched and blew crumbs all over Mr. Cox, who prayed silently for help. To anything that would listen.

Already, as they say in the papers, the situation was

deteriorating. Someone struck up on the tinkly piano for musical bumps, but the children were too excited to play properly. Those who were out refused to stay out, and tried to clobber the rest. By six o'clock, when the party was really due to start, Mrs. Cox (who was supposed to be pouring the drinks) was mopping the nose of a sobbing victim. She was muttering rude things about her husband for not keeping better order. Just then a buzz went round among the grown-up helpers. The conjurer had arrived, and was waiting in the church.

"What conjurer? Never knew we'd engaged a conjurer——" But Mr. Cox said: "All I know is, Mafeking has been relieved." Then he bawled for silence, and told the children to sit on the floor, as he had a surprise for them. Trevor, Larry and their gang shoved to the front. In the pointed doorway, a black figure was silhouetted against the faint glow from the lanterns. He beckoned it forward. The children raised a few cheers and cat-calls, the helpers clapped eagerly.

They saw a long, thin figure, dressed in an outfit that might have been hired from a theatre: frock coat, clerical collar, tall hat, white gloves, luxuriant ginger whiskers. He was wheeling a porter's trolley, which held a domed trunk of gleaming leather, with new brass handles, and "MAGIC" boldly painted on the lid.

It seemed to take the conjurer no time to reach the platform. There he turned and smiled down the hall in a vague, fixed way. Between the improbable whiskers, his face was very pink and white. The smile never left it, as he intoned in a sing-song tenor:

"Will someone assist me to elevate my magic box?"

The mob jostled round, and the trunk almost floated up by itself. Its owner bounded after it, with his arms folded, like a ballet dancer. The kids laughed and whistled, but some looked a little unnerved.

"If only his tricks are as good as he is," prayed Mr. Cox. "At least he's got them on his side."

But he spoke too soon. All the time this mystery conjurer was opening his trunk and taking out his stock-in-trade, the usual wand, scarves, goldfish bowl, folding screen and the like, the mobsters in the front row sniggered and scuffled. The first few card tricks were rather familiar. Larry kept explaining loudly how each one was done, while the others blew raspberries, or mimicked the conjurer's voice, which was certainly peculiar. The next row told them to belt up, whereupon they swivelled round and began to use their boots. Mr. Cox rolled up his sleeves. He'd hoped he wouldn't have to throw anybody out, but it seemed the time had come. Then an odd little headshake from the platform made him pause.

"For the next trick," smiled the conjurer, "I require two volunteers. For disappearing."

Some dear little girls stood up, but too late. Trevor and Larry had rushed the platform, more as if they were going to attack the conjurer than help him. Calmly he opened the trunk and bowed an invitation. They hesitated only for a moment. Then:

"Come on," said Trevor. "Let's bust 'is box for 'im an all."

"Watch me, here I come!" shrieked Larry.

They both jumped in heavily. Clearly they had no idea of allowing the lid to be shut on them. But something happened—whether they sank or were forced down, the audience could not see—but the conjurer was doing up the strap. He turned away, dusting his gloved hands, and began a series of quite brilliant tricks. The children were rivetted. They shouted: "Go on, Mister. Do another." Then, after about ten minutes, one of the front row stood up and asked, in a respectful tone such as he had probably

33

never used before, if Larry and Trevor could come out now, please?

"Bless my soul, I almost forgot." The conjurer opened the trunk, looked surprised, then tipped it towards the audience. Of course it was empty—an empty black cavern. Both children and grown-ups clapped frenziedly. Only Mr. Cox looked gloomy. He was certain that those boys would now emerge, leering, from somewhere quite different, under the platform or behind the curtain.

"Stop a minute, here's someone!" Their entertainer stooped and lifted out two rabbits, which he gave to the dear little girls. "Will these do?"

"YES!" roared the audience.

"No," protested some of the front row.

"One moment. Here are some more." Out came a kitten, a puppy, a flock of doves. Out came a small alligator— which he hastily dropped into the piano. Out came toys, rather good ones, for all the children. Little flames danced at the ends of the conjurer's fingers. He lifted his hat, and it rained chocolate drops. Then, bowing briefly, he tossed his equipment back into the trunk, and leapt from the platform.

"Now for tea," he cried. "And then some jolly games."

After this, the Blind Man's Buff, the guessing games and the dancing went like clockwork. The conjurer seemed to be everywhere at once, his black legs working like scissors, his whiskers flying No one noticed how the time was going until the caretaker appeared at the door, rattling his keys. The conjurer was prancing round the hall, astride an old mop, with the whole party following and joining in the chorus of some ancient song:

"Hey, hey, clear the way, here comes the Galloping Major!"

Mr. Cox stood looking on and wiping tears of laughter from his eyes. It was the best party he ever remembered.

34

The conjurer was prancing round the hall . . .

Suddenly his arm was disagreeably pinched, and a voice snarled: "Where's my Larry?"

It was Mrs. Murdoch, flashily dressed and flinty-faced, who seemed to be in a bad temper. "One of his mates came to fetch me. I was just having a drink with some friends. He said you'd sent him off somewhere. Well, I paid 10p for his ticket. He should be here."

Mr. Cox said: "Oh dear." He supposed the joke had gone far enough. He went up to the conjurer, who suddenly turned and headed for the platform. Mr. Cox stopped just where he was, and everything went black for a moment.

For he had been close enough to see that mask-like face sideways for the first time. And it really was a mask. The rim was visible behind the ear, and just above where the whisker began was a narrow gap. In that gap was— nothing.

When his sight cleared, the trunk was open. Trevor and Larry were scrambling out. He saw them slink down from the platform, both rather pinched and blue, as if with cold. Larry ran up to his mother and flung his arms round her. "Let's go home, Mum," he pleaded.

"Here, don't do that. Mind my good suit. What's the hurry? Didn't you enjoy the party?"

"Oh, yes, thank you, Mum——" His teeth chattered a bit. Then he caught Mr. Cox's eye, and dropped his gaze hurriedly. "And thank you too, Mr. Cox."

Trevor couldn't bring himself to say anything, but he shook hands, earnestly, for several seconds.

Wherever those boys had spent their evening, Mr. Cox was heartily glad he hadn't been with them.

Meanwhile the hall had almost emptied. The tall-hatted figure stood near the door, patting the last little heads as they went out. The thought of what might be inside those patting gloves turned Mr. Cox rather sick. But he felt that

36

he had had a lesson in minding his manners, and certainly someone ought to say thank you to—it.

But even as he hastened towards the door, the conjurer vanished into the church. The lanterns had mostly burned out, and the shadows hung over him, black and powerful. "Stop—er, stop a moment," he called waveringly. There were footfalls—oh, how he hoped they wouldn't turn back—and he caught the whisper of a song:

"Hey, hey—clear the way——"

He screwed up all his courage and ran along the aisle with a thumping heart. Here was the open church door, and the friendly street lamps. No one was in sight. Just the mass of the church against the sky, and the grave, stones that seemed to nod a little in the night wind.

"Excuse me, Mr. Cox——" called the caretaker, making him jump. He went back to the hall, where the clearing up was almost finished.

The old man was grumbling. "Now, sir, I must ask you to give me a hand with this here trunk. Why it should have been dragged out of the vestry and all the way along here into the hall, beats me. The vicar wouldn't half be wild if he knew——"

The trunk was very old, battered and dusty. Nothing was written on the lid. The caretaker swore it had lived in the vestry as long as he could remember. There was nothing inside but a few dead spiders.

During the next few weeks, a lot of people asked Mr. Cox how he had got hold of the marvellous conjurer. He found he couldn't tell them the truth. After all, he was a bank manager, with a reputation to keep up, and he didn't want them to think he was mad. So he pretended, even to his wife, that it was just a local man who had rung up at the last minute and offered to come. Unfortunately he hadn't given his address.

In the spring, the demolition company moved into the

street, which echoed with the crash of falling masonry. St. Ethelburga's vanished forever, and a lot of surprised-looking sky appeared in the gap.

Mr. Cox felt sad. He went to the archives department in the local library and read up all he could about the church. His heart beat a little faster when he found an old Parish Magazine, with an account of a Ladies' Evening in 1882, presided over by the curate, the Reverend Francis Wherry. "His humorous songs," it said, "will make him the life and soul of any party ever to be held in this hall." Did he sing them 'The Galloping Major'? There was nothing about that. And if he was a conjurer as well, it didn't say so.

Disappointed, Mr. Cox yielded to temptation at last, and confessed the whole story to his wife. But she wasn't much help either. She said she didn't remember enough to know if he was telling the truth, or had just dreamt it all, and the only merciful things about children's parties is the way you forget them.

At least Larry and Trevor were different boys ever afterwards. Everyone noticed it. When last I heard of them, both had joined the Venture Scouts, and were considered an ornament to their troop.

A CAT ON THE DRIVE

by Brian Morse

WE'D been in the new house only three days when we noticed that with it we'd acquired something out of the ordinary.

We were on our way back from the station where we'd been to pick up Mum off the London train. She'd been home—to our old house, that is, a house in a quiet street near the largest park in Barnet—to clear up some outstanding business with the solicitor. As Dad drove through the dark, unfamiliar streets we asked her questions about our old neighbours—had she had time to go and visit any of them? Had she bumped into any of our friends? And, particularly, was there any news of our cat, Tibby, which had disappeared within five minutes of the furniture removers' arrival and which we'd had to leave behind? Mum had been able to speak to a few of our neighbours, and she'd seen two of Tracy's friends, but of Tibby she had no news at all. Mrs. Elam, who'd been our next-door neighbour, had promised to phone if the cat did turn up.

As we neared the new house—The Laurels, Church Lane—we all fell silent. We drove down a street of shops, where lighted windows shone on to empty pavements, turned right into a lane that led under a railway bridge, skirted the Green, a wide open space of grass, and so into Church Lane. The Laurels was on a bend, and as the car turned right its lights swept across the front of the house.

"This isn't home," Tracy suddenly said. "I don't think it ever will be."

"Of course it will," Mum said soothingly. "It's new to us yet. You wait."

We all knew Tracy was thinking of the inseparable friends she had spent so much of her time with back in Barnet. It had been worst of all for Tracy, pulling up her roots—much worse than for me. I was five years older than her and had welcomed the change.

"Michael—will you open the gates?" Dad said.

I jumped out of the car and did as he'd said. As I finished and was signalling him to come on I thought that our first night here had been exciting because the house was new, and the second night too, but that tonight it was just an ordinary house with no real character of its own.

39

It looked gloomy, uninhabited. I stepped back as Dad turned the car into the drive and it was then that I saw a cat. It was sitting stock-still in the middle of the drive, staring straight into the oncoming lights. It didn't as much as move a whisker as the car approached it.

I began to shout—I thought for a fraction of a second it might be Tibby—but it was too late. Just as the bumper reached it and obscured my view, Dad put on the brakes. I looked for where the cat had gone to, but I could see no sign of it at all.

"Why did you stop so suddenly?" I heard Mum asking.

"A cat," Dad said. He wound the window down and, peering out, said to me, "I didn't hit it, did I? I hope not. I didn't feel a bump."

"You must have done," I said. "I didn't see it run off." I nipped round, but there was no cat on the drive in front of the car, nor when I knelt down could I see anything underneath. "Nothing, Dad," I said, straightening up. "Perhaps it managed to slip away under the car without us noticing."

"Perhaps." Dad hesitated, as if he wasn't totally convinced that even a cat could have been as agile as that. He'd been travelling at quite a speed. Then he told me to shut the gates and drove the car up in front of the house.

The cat had obviously disappeared, so we thought nothing more about it till we were going in through the front door and Tracy called out:

"There's a cat on the drive again."

We looked.

"That's the cat," Dad said. "The one I nearly hit." A car was coming round the corner at that moment so we saw it clearly, a great tabby, proud and disdainful. "What a whopper," Dad said.

"Tibby wouldn't like that one," Tracy said. "No wonder she didn't want to come here."

"What on earth do you mean?" Dad said, but Tracy had already stepped into the hall.

I went back down the drive while Dad unloaded something from the boot. It was pitch-dark, but another car came sweeping round the corner and I saw the cat again. It must have sensed me coming for it stood up, glanced in my direction and stalked towards the shadows and melted away. Suddenly I felt cold and lonely. On an impulse I rushed headlong towards the house.

"What's up?" said Dad as I panted to a halt beside him.

"Nothing," I said, feeling foolish and avoiding his searching eyes. Yet, though I could see no reason why, I had felt scared.

Mum phoned Mrs. Elam every other day from then on, but Tibby didn't reappear. The new people, Mrs. Elam said, were settling in fine. How were we? Fine too, Mum said, but that wasn't exactly true. It was hard to put a finger on the reason why, but we still felt ill at ease in The Laurels—and the feeling wasn't passing. There was nothing sinister about it, but it wasn't a happy house. Not that I had much time to think about that, for I was busy going to my new school and making new friends, exploring our surroundings and generally finding out what there was to do. Nor would I have given that cat a second thought, except one night Dad came in late and the first thing he said was: "Every time I arrive here between eight and nine there's that cat sitting there on the drive as bold as can be, glaring into my headlights. And do you think it will move out of the way until I'm virtually on top of it? It seems to think it owns the place. The funny thing is, I never see where it slips away to. You remember that night I thought I'd knocked it over, don't you?"

I'd just finished my homework and was watching T.V.,

but curiosity made me go to the window and push aside the curtains. It was a moonlit night, the garden was full of deep shadows and unearthly patches of light, and, as Dad had said, there was the cat brooding on the drive. Suddenly, as though I were doing something brave—but why should it have been brave?—I decided to go out and investigate. I slipped out of the room, slung my coat on and issued forth into the night.

The cat turned its head as I stepped out into the porch. I hesitated, then walked towards it, expecting it to slip away, but no, this time it didn't. It stretched out its front paws luxuriously, as if it had been sitting there for an hour and not for just the few minutes since Dad had brought the car in, then took a hopping step towards me. I couldn't be sure, but it seemed to me to be lame in one of its back legs. Its eyes were on me now, large and mournful, catching diamond points of light from the lamp on the porch. Suddenly I hesitated again. I felt distinctly scared —but of a cat? I tried to control my rising panic. I was sweating, though it was a bitter late October night. Then a wave of cold swept through my body.

The cat took another hopping step towards me, and sat down again It cocked its ears, hearing voices behind me from the partially-open hall door. I was inclined to run back to those friendly voices, but something in the cat's look pulled me those ten remaining yards. I stooped down beside it.

"Hallo, pussy," I said.

I put my hand out to stroke it from the crown of its head, which it had lifted for my caress, down its arching back to its tail, which was moving slightly from side to side, but my hand encountered nothing, passing through where the cat stood. Doubting my senses, I tried it again, but the result was the same. The cat just wasn't there.

For a long moment I stooped, unable to move. Whether I was paralysed by fear or by surprise I couldn't judge. The cat, too, must have sensed something was wrong, for it moved closer to me, running its head and side against my trouser legs, turning and turning with a hopping jump about my ankles. But it couldn't touch me, just as I couldn't touch it. Suddenly I stepped back, and as I did so the cat looked up at me piteously and gave a plaintive miaow—except I could only imagine it, not hear it.

I might have stood there for ever staring into its sad eyes, but at that moment the clock on the church tower down the road began to strike. The cat turned and, giving what I imagined to be a shrug of resignation, stalked towards the bushes. As it passed through a patch of bright moonlight it vanished, vanished into thin air. One moment it was there, the next it wasn't. I was left with a sense of desolation far far stronger than I'd ever experienced. For a moment I felt as if I'd added ten years to my life. I turned towards the house and for a fraction of a second I had the impression that our new house was in flames. I blinked, and the house was still there, intact, the light in the lounge softened by the curtains. But the image had been real enough.

Back in the house I was evasive about why I'd been outside, which irritated Mum and Dad, who didn't like us being mysterious, but it was Tracy's bed time so they didn't press the point. Tracy's so much trouble to get upstairs Mum had her hands completely full, and Dad had some work to finish for his office. However, as I went up to bed myself a little later, Tracy, who should have been asleep, called me into her room.

"It was the cat," she said, "wasn't it? It upset you. There's something wrong with it."

I tried to put her fears to rest, but Tracy wasn't having any of it. Perhaps, being the age she was, she was more

sensitive to anything that had to do with the supernatural.

"This house is haunted," she said flatly.

"What have you seen, then?" I asked, giving myself
away immediately by the urgency of my question.

"Nothing," she said, " and I don't think I will. But it's
half-haunted, as if 'they' were trying to break through and
can't. That's why Tibby won't come near it," she added.
"She knew what it was like before we came."

I argued the point, saying Tibby had been scared by
the furniture-removers, but I couldn't change her mind.
She said cats were more sensitive than us and Tibby had
immediately sensed, after Mum's and Dad's visits of in-
spection to The Laurels, that it was no place for her.

The next day Dad unwittingly provided the clue I wanted.
As you can guess, the ghost-cat had made me a little bit
nervous. My mind was running round in circles to try and
discover why it should be haunting our drive and garden.

Mum had just said that she'd noticed our house was
the newest in Church Lane. All the others were at least
twenty years older, she said. Why was that?

"Why? Didn't I tell you?" Dad said. "There was a
house here before this one. It was bombed during the last
war, in 1941. The one we're living in was built in 1948."

"I never knew they bombed here," I said. "There's no
industry, just houses."

"Well, they didn't," Dad said. "It was just one of those
unlucky things. A German plane must have got off course,
seen lights, and dropped an odd bomb it had left while it
was flying back to base. It was even unluckier the bomb
was on target. Apparently the people who lived here were
prosecuted more than once for not observing the black-
out."

"Who told you?" I asked, my voice suddenly sharp.

"What was his name? Yes, a Mr. Tucker," Dad said. "His house is next to the church. I got into conversation with him one day when I was up here scouting around for somewhere to live. He was a friend of the people who lived here. I can tell you one thing, though. The date the bomb fell was Guy Fawkes' Night. Quite an irony."

November 5th was the Wednesday of the next week.

Cycling home on Monday I noticed a man walking down the path of the house next to the church. On an impulse I stopped and waited for him to reach the road. He was oldish, retired I would have said, and had a cheerful expression about his face that made me willing to ask him a question.

As he saw me looking at him he smiled and said hallo.

"We're living at The Laurels," I said.

"Oh yes? I must have met your father then," he replied. "We had an interesting chat."

"The people who lived there when it was bombed—did they have a big tabby cat?"

"A cat?" he said, looking at me strangely. "Yes, they did."

"And was it hurt by the bomb?"

"Why yes," he said. "It hung around the ruins days after, hopping on one leg. No one could get near it, though. It was rather pitiful. You'd expect a dog to be upset by that kind of thing, but not so much a cat. Anyway, how on earth did you know about that?"

I covered up. "It's just my sister. She reckons she's got sixth sense. Our own cat, Tibby, disappeared before we made the move, and she says it's because the cat knew there was something odd about the house."

Mr. Tucker scratched his head. "People don't like living in the new house, that's true. It must have changed hands more than a dozen times in the last twenty years. But I've never heard of any ghosts. That's what you're talking about, isn't it—ghosts?''

As best I could, I reassured him that that wasn't true, for Mum and Dad wouldn't have thanked me if a rumour like that about our house had got around the neighbourhood, and took my leave.

Bonfire night was cloudless. We let off our fireworks beneath a starry sky with a half-moon glimmering down near the horizon. Our bonfire was in the back garden, so at about a quarter to nine I pretended to have to go into the house, but instead went straight through the hall and out of the front door. The cat was there, sitting as it always did on the drive down near the gates. I walked towards it without hesitation, and it turned to meet me as if I were an old friend. By now we were used to each other, for most nights I'd been able to slip out and give it what comfort I could during its endless vigil. It seemed to me the loneliest creature in the world. How could one get used to caressing and petting an animal that wasn't there? Somehow, if it were humanly possible, I'd done it, though a shiver of apprehension always ran through me as I put out my fingers to touch—and couldn't touch it.

The cat was restless that night. The reason was obvious. Apart from the fact that it was the anniversary of its owners' deaths, the fireworks at the back of the house must have upset it considerably. It prowled to and fro in front of me, hobbling back to my fingers every now and then, but too nervous to stay put. As time went by it became more and more nervous, till at last it stood stock-still, staring at the house. I looked too, but saw nothing.

I went to crouch by it. The cat didn't move, nor did it have any reaction to the caresses I tried to lay on its head and back. It just stared at the house.

Then, suddenly, I was aware that I could no longer see

our house. An older, more old-fashioned building stood in its place, and in the star-lit sky I could hear a plane—far off, but coming nearer.

The house was dark, but all of a sudden a door at the side opened and, in a blaze of light, a proud tabby cat stepped out into the garden. By now the plane was very near, and I could see its silhouetted shape against the stars. Then it was above us, and I could hear the whistle of something falling towards us. I ducked and instinctively pulled the cat close to my body. There was an explosion. The house seemed to rock and then crumble. It burst into flames, and the tabby struggled in my arms to get away.

For a moment it was real. I could touch it. I tried to soothe it with my hands, oblivious to the inferno twenty yards in front of me. Then a cat, the image of the one I was holding, dragged itself painfully past us into the bushes. I looked down into my arms and saw I was holding nothing. I looked up and saw only the house into which we'd just moved. Stunned, I heard the telephone ringing, but could not gather my wits together to go and answer it. I knew, however, it was Mrs. Elam phoning to say that Tibby had been found, safe and well. I knew too that though the tabby was for ever gone, I would be haunted by its sadness for the rest of my life.

PORTRAIT OF RHODA

by Lucy Norris

"Oh, Sarah, it's beautiful!" chorused Lorna and Irene Edwards, gazing with wide-eyed admiration at the roomy four-poster bed with its dainty silken drapes. "Are we really going to sleep in it tonight?"

Lorna and Irene were identical twins and often spoke in unison. Sarah Parker smiled fondly at them. "But of course you are," she confirmed. "When I invite my best friends home for Christmas I try to grant their every wish. You said you wanted to sleep in a four-poster; and so you shall."

"Good old Sarah," said Lorna, giving her a pat on the back. "We really are grateful to you. When Mummy fell ill we faced the prospect of a dreary Christmas with Aunt Edna. Instead, here we are living in the lap of luxury." She swept her hand around the room. "I know you told us you lived in a family mansion, but we didn't expect anything as fantastic as this."

"It is a lovely old house, isn't it?" said Sarah with justifiable pride. "It was built by my great-great-grand-father, Mortimer Parker; and Parkers have lived here ever since. My father was born in that bed."

"How romantic," sighed the twins.

Sarah glanced at her wrist watch. "Good, it's teatime. I'm starving. Come on you two, I smell crumpets cooking. Lovely, lovely crumpets with oodles of butter and honey."

"You're supposed to be on a diet," Lorna reminded her as Sarah led the way down to the lounge. "You boasted to Avril Sinclair you would lose half a stone in weight before next term."

"I know I did," admitted Sarah, "but I wasn't feeling hungry at the time." She sighed enviously. "You two don't know how lucky you are to be slim."

"We wouldn't be if we ate as much as you do," said Irene bluntly, but not unkindly. "I'll be your conscience for the next three weeks, Sarah. Every time you start to over-eat I will stop you. Agreed?"

Sarah looked down at her plump figure and then at Irene's slim one. "Agreed," she said with misgivings, as she led them into the lounge where her mother **was** waiting to serve tea in front of a roaring log fire.

Mrs. Parker welcomed them and began to hand round dainty china plates. "I'm sure you girls are hungry after your journey here." She smiled at the twins. "Lorna dear, help yourself to a crumpet, or would you prefer buttered toast?"

Sarah gave a little giggle. "That's Irene, Mummy."

Mrs. Parker looked from one twin to the other and shook her head. "You are so alike. I don't think I shall ever be able to tell you apart."

"It's quite simple really, Mummy," laughed Sarah. "Irene parts her hair on the right; Lorna's is parted on the left. L for Lorna and L for left. And to make it even easier for you, Irene will be the one who keeps frowning and tut-tutting each time I reach for a second helping of anything."

Irene certainly kept an eagle eye on Sarah. By the time they went to bed that night Sarah was convinced she had already lost weight.

Lorna awoke some hours later to find a bright beam of light shining straight into her eyes, dazzling her. Before she could call out, a hand pressed down over her mouth and a voice whispered:

"It's all right, Lorna. It's only me."

The hand was removed from her mouth and Lorna hissed angrily: "Really, Sarah, if this is your idea of a joke . . ."

"No, honestly, I wasn't trying to frighten you," whispered Sarah. The light from the small torch she carried threw strange shadows on to her face, giving her a peculiar, grotesque expression.

"What were you doing, then?"

Sarah raised a warning finger to her lips. "Please don't wake Irene," she pleaded. "She wouldn't understand."

"Understand what?"

"That I won't get a wink of sleep tonight unless I have something to eat."

"But it's the middle of the night," complained Lorna. "Everyone's in bed asleep."

"I know that," nodded Sarah. "That's why I want you to come down to the kitchen with me. I'm too scared to go alone. Be a sport, Lorna. I'd do the same for you."

Lorna was about to refuse when she remembered that if it hadn't been for Sarah's kindness, she and her sister would be spending a miserable Christmas with Aunt Edna.

"Oh, all right," she agreed, slipping silently out of bed to avoid waking Irene. Pulling on her dressing-gown, she tip-toed after a jubilant Sarah.

They made their way by the light of the torch but, once downstairs, Sarah switched on the hall light, and together the girls ran along to the kitchen. It wasn't until Lorna stepped on to the cold, flagged kitchen floor that she realised she had forgotten to put on her slippers.

"Do hurry up," she pleaded as Sarah rummaged through a large cupboard, opening a variety of tins. "My feet are frozen. What are you looking for, anyway?"

"That chocolate fudge cake Irene wouldn't let me have at teatime," replied Sarah, licking her lips in anticipation.

Lorna hopped from one foot to the other. "A plain biscuit would be less fattening," she said reprovingly. "I dread to think what Irene will say when you tell her you've been guzzling a cake in the middle of the night."

"I have no intention of telling her," replied Sarah. She wrenched the lid from yet another tin. "Aha! Success at last! Like a piece?"

"No, I wouldn't. And please hurry. I'm cold."

Sarah found a knife and helped herself to a slice of the

cake. "Sure you won't have some?" she enquired before putting the tin away.

"Quite sure," Lorna said firmly. Her eyes widened as she caught sight of the generous slice Sarah was holding. "If you eat that you'll not only get fatter but you'll come out in spots as well," she warned.

"You're probably right," agreed Sarah comfortably, "but it will be worth it." She took a large bite and sighed blissfully.

Lorna regarded Sarah's bulging cheeks with disgust. "May we go back to bed now?" she asked hopefully.

"When I've eaten this," Sarah said with some difficulty, speaking out of the side of her mouth. "If you're feeling cold, we can sit in Dad's study. He always has a fire half-way up the chimney so I'm sure it won't have burnt out yet."

It hadn't. In fact, the firelight was so bright they didn't bother to put the room light on, but curled up on the thick furry rug and, while Sarah contentedly ate her cake, Lorna warmed her icy toes.

"If only I didn't like sweet things it would be so easy to diet," sighed Sarah between mouthfuls. "You won't tell Irene about this little indiscretion, will you?"

Lorna didn't answer. She was gazing intently at a life-size portrait of a young and very beautiful lady holding a red rose in her hand. The portrait was on the wall opposite the fireplace and in the flickering light the painting looked most life-like.

"Isn't she beautiful!" exclaimed Lorna. "Who is she?"

"Her name was Rhoda, which is Greek for rose," replied Sarah. "During her lifetime she kept vases of roses in her room all summer long and always wore a rose-scented perfume."

"Was she a relation of yours?"

"Wish she had been," sighed Sarah, "then I might have

inherited some of her beauty. On the other hand, knowing my luck, I would probably have inherited her vile temper instead."

"Did she have a temper?" Lorna studied the sweetly-smiling face. "I find that hard to believe."

"So did my grandfather, Henry Parker," sniffed Sarah. "He met Rhoda Marston when she was eighteen. They met at a hunt ball and he fell head over heels in love with her. At first he refused to believe the stories he was told about her temper but it wasn't long before he found out for himself.

"Henry had arranged to go riding with Rhoda but had to cancel this when his mother asked him to act as host in his father's absence. Henry explained his problem to Rhoda but she insisted he should keep his date with her."

"What happened?" asked Lorna.

"What didn't happen!" Sarah rolled her eyes dramatically. "That evening when Henry and his mother were seated with their guests at dinner, they heard a horse galloping. It was Rhoda, riding at breakneck speed across the lawn. When she reached the terrace she halted the sweating beast and shouted for Henry. The french windows to the dining room were open—it being a hot night—and she could see Henry sitting at the table.

"Henry's youngest sister, Clare, was present at the dinner party and she wrote a full account of the affair in her diary; that's how we know all about it," said Sarah, fortifying herself with the last mouthful of cake. "When Rhoda shouted for him, Henry turned very white but continued to entertain his guests. Rhoda grew more and more angry and—you'll never believe this—she actually rode her horse up the terrace steps and in through the open french doors. Imagine it! She actually rode into the dining room! Rhoda's horse, Magic, reared and pranced before the astonished diners while Rhoda, her long hair cascading wildly around her shoulders, struck at Henry with her riding whip."

"Poor Henry," exclaimed Lorna.

Sarah nodded. "Clare wrote that he behaved magnificently. In spite of the danger from the horse's hooves, to say nothing of the whip, he caught hold of Magic's bridle and tried to soothe the frightened creature.

"Rhoda was furious. She screamed at Henry to leave her horse alone, and struck at him again. The horse reared and bumped against the table, knocking several wine glasses to the floor. The glasses were part of a family heirloom. Rhoda knew this and laughed with pleasure. She cried: 'I'll teach you to break a date with me!' then leant forward and swept several more from the table with her whip."

Sarah lowered her voice to a stage whisper.

"And then the most awful thing happened . . ."

"What?" gulped Lorna.

"Rhoda's horse, frightened by the smashing glass, reared suddenly. Rhoda lost her balance and was thrown to the ground, and . . . the most terrible thing . . . one of the horse's hooves struck her face, cutting deeply across her left cheek.

"Rhoda went hysterical. She grabbed a knife from the table and attempted to slash at Henry, but by now the horrified guests had gathered their wits sufficiently to come to his aid. Rhoda was carried screaming from the room and taken home. She was kept under sedation for weeks."

"What about her face?" asked Lorna as Sarah paused to lick the last crumbs from her fingers. "Was she badly scarred?"

"Hideously so," said Sarah with almost ghoulish delight. "She refused to go out or allow anyone to visit her. Apart from her family, the only person to see her after the accident was the artist who painted that portrait."

"Was that painted after the accident?" asked Lorna.

"Yes. That's why she has turned her head so that you can't see the left side of her face. Rhoda heard about a wandering artist—some say he was a gipsy but, whatever he was, he claimed he could paint a person's soul into their portrait. Rhoda had him paint that portrait of her and when, a year later, Henry married Isobelle Richmond, Rhoda sent him that painting as a wedding present.

"There's poor taste for you! Poor old Henry married to a plain-looking but sweet-tempered girl and Rhoda sends him that gorgeous portrait of herself. They say Isobelle was very upset, so Henry put the painting in here—and here it has remained ever since."

"What happened to Rhoda?"

"Oh, yes. I nearly forgot to tell you the best bit! After sending Henry that painting, Rhoda killed herself! She plunged a dagger into her heart and with her dying breath she cursed poor Henry and vowed he too should meet a violent death.

"And he did! A year to the day after Rhoda died, Henry was found murdered: in this very room!"

Lorna gave a gasp of horror and began to shake all over. Sarah regarded her with amusement.

"You've never struck me as the nervous type," she observed dryly.

"I'm not," Lorna shivered. "I don't know what's the matter with me, honestly I don't. I have the most terrible feeling that something awful is going to happen. Tell me, Sarah. Who murdered Henry?"

Sarah shrugged. "They never found out. Poor Henry was slumped back in that chair, a stab wound in his chest. His eyes were wide open and the expression on his face was one of—well, horror, they say. Clare wrote in her diary that she believed *she* knew who had murdered Henry but that no one would believe her."

"Who did she think it was?" asked Lorna, rising to her feet, her face as white as chalk.

"She didn't say," shrugged Sarah. "I think we ought to go back to bed now, don't you?"

Lorna stared up at the portrait. "She did it!" she said positively. "She killed Henry."

Sarah looked at Lorna in surprise. "You're talking nonsense. Rhoda had been dead a year when it happened. How could she have done it?"

Lorna's face was very pale, her body shaking all over. She spoke in small sobs. "Show us how you did it, Rhoda," she gasped. "Show us, I dare you!"

To Sarah's horror the painted head moved, turned and stared down at them. A look of intense hatred shone in the vivid blue eyes; a hatred directed at Lorna. The figure rose and stepped from the frame. Sarah heard the rustle of the stiff silk dress; saw the hideous scar. An overpowering, almost suffocating scent came from the red rose in Rhoda's hand.

Terrified, the two girls clung to each other, mesmerised with fear and unable to protect themselves.

From the folds of the silken gown the slim white hand withdrew a small dagger. Menacingly, she advanced towards them, the hand raised ready to strike.

In the shadows of the doorway behind her a scream rang out. Rhoda swung round and gave a startled cry when she saw Irene standing there. Irene, pale and shaking, continued to scream again and again.

Rhoda stared from one twin to the other. The sight of identical girls standing either side of the room seemed to bewilder her and she backed away.

Sarah, jerked into action by the screams, pulled Lorna across the room. Lights were switched on all over the house as disturbed sleepers rose from their beds to investigate the noise. Grabbing the twins, Sarah ran from the

The figure rose and stepped from the frame . . .

study and along the hallway. At the foot of the stairs they collided with Sarah's father.

Trembling, sobbing, they told him what had happened.

"Something woke me up," cried Irene. "I found Lorna was not in bed and I knew, I just knew she was in danger somewhere, so I came to look for her."

"And if Irene hadn't screamed when she did, Rhoda would have killed us," cried Sarah. "As it was, I nearly died of fright when Rhoda stepped from that picture frame."

"This I must see for myself," said Mr. Parker. He strode towards his study, followed, at a safe distance, by the three nervous girls.

Switching on the light he walked in. The girls peered cautiously in from the doorway. The portrait was as it had always been. Rhoda Marston gazed gently down, a smile on her lips, a look of innocence in her painted eyes.

"But I don't understand . . ." exclaimed Sarah.

Mr. Parker smiled kindly. "When you told Rhoda's story to Lorna, it started her imagination working. Somehow, Lorna made you believe it was possible for a painting to come to life, and then you both let your imagination run riot."

"But what about Irene?" persisted Sarah. "She didn't know about Rhoda, yet she saw her."

"Telepathy," said Mr. Parker in that matter-of-fact way of grown-ups. "It's a well-known fact that people—especially twins—can transmit thoughts to each other, even when many miles apart. Lorna imagined the portrait was alive and put the idea into Irene's mind. Now girls, back to bed. In the morning, Sarah, I would like an explanation as to why you and Lorna were downstairs at all."

"So would I," hissed Irene as they trundled upstairs. "What were you two doing, anyway?"

"Don't tell her, Lorna," said Sarah, brightening considerably as an idea occurred to her. "Let her guess!" She beamed upon Irene. "Lorna will send you the answer by telepathy! Imagine the fun we can have!"

"No, thanks," exclaimed Irene. "I've had quite enough imagining for one night."

"I suppose we did imagine it all," said Lorna. "I mean, a painting couldn't really come to life . . . Could it?"

"I guess not," sighed Sarah. "Pity. It would have made a smashing story to tell the girls at school."

Downstairs in the study a red rose petal lay un-noticed on the floor beneath the portrait. A rose petal as garden-fresh as the day it had been picked.

And red roses don't grow in December.

THE TOCKLEY FAMILIAR

by KAY LEITH

NORTH THROCTON was a dead little place, especially at the beginning of October. If it had had any visitors that summer they were long since gone, leaving it to sink back into somnolence—if, indeed, it had ever wakened up.

The first week hadn't been too bad. Derek had met the son of a doctor and they'd done a bit of fishing, but since then there had been nobody around who was less than double his thirteen years.

His aunt, the only member of the family free to take Derek on a late holiday, spent a lot of her time visiting local museums and churches and discussing her expeditions with another spinster with similar interests whom she'd met through the vicar.

For this Derek was grateful, for Aunt Greta was inclined to be a mite tedious about gravestones, brass rubbings and ancient parish records, and impatient with people who didn't share her mania.

As the second week began, Derek wondered if he might be driven, out of boredom, to doing just that! He'd exhausted the possibilities of the rocky coast, and there wasn't a street or alley in the neat and tidy North Throcton that he hadn't explored.

One day he walked beyond the small town, past the golf course and up the slight hill towards a wooded area. There wasn't much of interest except the fields and grazing farm animals, until about half a mile out, when he found a narrow road which didn't have any "Private—Keep Out" notices.

The grass had grown through the surface in the middle of the road, which proved that it wasn't used much. He decided to investigate. If anyone asked him what he was doing there, he could honestly say that he didn't know he was trespassing.

There were pine trees on the right, over the wire fence, and a field on the left. Round the first bend he stopped, startled. In his path was a furtive-looking, middle-aged man who seemed even more surprised than Derek was himself.

"Excuse me," said Derek. "Am I trespassing, do you know?"

The man, who had a sack over his shoulder, said: "Well, if you be, I be, too!"

"Does the road go anywhere?"

"As far as Tockley House, what's left of it, but I wouldn't advise you to go there." The man put down his sack, lit a pipe and blew out clouds of pungent smoke. " 'Tain't a good place."

The boy was immediately intrigued. "What do you mean?"

59

"Well, lad, 'tain't a place to go after dusk—or daylight neither! Nobody lives there no more, but things happen."

"What kind of things? Has anything ever happened to you?"

"Off an' on," said the man. "Favourite silly game is throwing stones."

"But, if nobody lives there, it must be somebody from the town playing a joke."

"I'd like to catch 'im then, whoever he is. I'd give him stones, an' no mistake!" The man picked up his sack. "You'd best come back along the road wi' me, lad."

Derek shook his head. "Thanks all the same, Mr . . .?"

"John Biddle—general odd-job man and one-time thatcher."

"I'm Derek Waverley, Mr. Biddle. I think I'll go and have a look at the house, since I've come this far."

"Well, it's up to you, Derek. But only look, mind. Don't go near the pesky place."

"All right, Mr. Biddle."

The tumbled towers of Tockley House came into sight a quarter of a mile further on, standing on a slight hill. The gaunt rubble, in some parts, seemed like a disease disfiguring the pleasant scene, whereas in other sections smothering ivy made it appear almost as if the house were still whole and occupied. There were traces, as Derek noted as he edged closer, of what had once been formal and graceful gardens. Sweeping oaks and beeches stood in the spacious, unkempt parkland, and there was a long, curving, weed-covered drive. A broken fountain stood in front of the house.

Derek stood looking up at the ruin. In spite of its bleak and baleful aspect, it was, after all, just an old tumbled-down house—the kind where one wouldn't be surprised if there were treasures buried somewhere within its walls.

60

The people who had lived there must have been very rich.

John Biddle had said not to go near the place, but what did he mean by "near"—ten yards, twenty yards, or what?

There wasn't any sound anywhere except the faint chirp of birds, and Derek started to walk slowly up the drive. He had just reached the fountain when a piece of brick came hurtling through the air and missed him by inches. He stopped, fighting the desire to turn and run.

What made him move forward again was the idea that someone somewhere in the ruins probably thought that it was funny to scare the daylights out of people. Like John Biddle, he'd give him "stones" if he caught him— that is, if it wouldn't be more prudent to run! It all depended on his size!

The front door had long rotted and fallen in, and only one square column remained of the portico. Through the gap Derek could see the heaps of weed-shrouded rubble.

This time, as he was within ten feet of the gaping door, not one stone but several began to rain about him. Making a quick decision, and shielding his head, he ran for the ivied wall and crouched with his back to it. His heart was hammering like a steam press now, and uppermost in his mind was the problem of how he was going to get back down the drive again unscathed if the stone-throwing didn't stop.

"Come on out!" he shouted. "Don't hide yourself like a coward!"

That let loose a fury of stones, as if all the spirits of the air were affronted by the accusation. They rattled all around him, striking his head and arms. Luckily the ones that hit him weren't very big—just enough to leave a small bruise. However, the odd thing was that they were coming from all directions, as though an army of urchins, spread around the grounds, were using him for target practice. But there was absolutely no sign of any living creature.

"Who are you?" Derek shouted.

As quickly as they'd begun, the stones suddenly stopped. The place grew as quiet as a mausoleum. The boy moved away from the wall slowly, ready to dive back to cover at the first hint of another fusillade.

Nerves jumping, he looked up at the gaping windows, and then, eyes searching, went through into what had been the entrance hall of the old place. There was no roof at all, not a single slate or joist still in position, and Derek wondered if Tockley House had originally been burned down.

Suddenly there was a tremendous crash, and he spun round. Where he'd been standing only a moment before lay the remains of a coping stone. It was patently impossible for any human being to get up there, knock off the stone, and then hide—not unless he knew how to fly!

It occurred to Derek that it might have been pure coincidence—that the coping stone had required no help to push it free—but if he wanted to believe that he would be very naïve.

"All right," he said aloud. "I can take a hint. I'll go."

The hairs on his neck prickled and his muscles twitched with strain as he determinedly and slowly stepped over the shattered coping stone and walked down the curving drive. He looked back before the house was lost to sight, but no jeering figure, or visible ghostly manifestation, watched his retreat. Yet, there was someone or something there at Tockley House—something very odd indeed . . .

Aunt Greta was in a mood at dinner. "A little knowledge is a dangerous thing! Some people imagine, because they know a little, that they know it all! It's so tiresome!"

Derek surmised that she must have had a difference

of opinion with someone. Her spinster friend, for instance?

"There's a big ruin not far from here," said Derek temptingly. "I shouldn't be surprised if it has some interesting lore connected with it. I'd ask at the Town Hall, only they're inclined not to take people my age seriously . . ."

"Hmmm. That's true," said his aunt. "Old, you say, and ruined? What's its name again? Hmmm. Yes. Well, I've got some time on my hands tomorrow. I'll find out what I can for you."

Derek was drawn back to Tockley House next day, as though someone were pulling a string. He supposed it was the lure of the unexplainable, and until he'd found out what was going on, he didn't think he'd get much peace.

He stood about twenty yards away, looking and wondering. The place seemed to taunt him. He moved forward, and out of nowhere a jagged stone whizzed through the air and struck him above the eye.

Blood pouring down his face, he ran towards the house, hurt and furious. His handkerchief quickly became soaked.

"Come out, you coward!" he shouted to the uncaring walls. "Coward! Coward! Coward!"

His voice reverberated defiantly. "Coward! Coward! Come out! Beastly coward!"

There was a distinct tremor in the air, which the boy sensed, as though something were responding to his shouts.

"Beast!" He listened, walking forward slowly. "Beastly coward! Beast!"

It was a mere whisper at first, like a faint rumble, but it grew and swelled and expanded until an angry gale was born. It howled in and out of the vacant windows, bent the ivy, flattened the mounds of weeds, roused the derelict dust into eye-stinging spitefulness.

Derek crouched on elbows and knees before the portico, his hands and forearms shielding his head. The wind was filling his nostrils with grit, and it even got under his closed eyelids.

He lost track of time in the buffetting of the wind and the cuffs and slaps he received from unknown objects flung along by the force of the gale. Eventually it seemed to him that it was lessening, and he opened his eyes and looked up. His blood froze with horror.

About four feet above the top step floated two coral-red slits! They stayed the same distance apart all the time and seemed like eyes. They bored right down into the boy's brain, and sweat broke out all over his body.

Derek knew then what it must feel like to be a rabbit mesmerised by a snake. He could not move! The eyes came nearer until they floated directly above him. He cringed, terrified.

Then, like a puff of smoke, they were gone!

For nearly ten minutes he remained crouched, utterly shattered, afraid to move. What was it he had seen? Certainly nothing human—nor animal either! A ghostly guardian, perhaps ... The guardian of Tockley House?

But what was it guarding? Treasure? There seemed no other way to account for it.

Feeling dazed and shaken, Derek got to his feet. It was quiet and peaceful now, but at any moment the stones might start to fly, or the thing decide to return, so as quickly as his trembling legs would take him, he dashed directly across the weed-choked debris and down the drive.

He found his aunt in her favourite tea-room, having coffee with an old lady. Aunt Greta quizzed him about the sticking plaster on his forehead, but he'd already thought up a good excuse.

"This is Mrs. Terence, Derek, and she's the owner of Tockley House."

Derek looked at Mrs. Terence with renewed interest and shook her hand. "There's something odd about the house, isn't there, Mrs. Terence?"

The old lady nodded, then described how her family had tried to re-build the house after the fire, but each time they'd had to abandon the project because the workmen wouldn't stay. It had acquired a bad reputation and even local farmers refused to graze farm animals on the land.

"As you can imagine," said Mrs. Terence. "Not being able to sell it has meant great hardship for us. Grandfather Allan Broadfoot spent most of his money building the place, and when it was destroyed we were left almost destitute. From what I have been able to piece together from faint personal knowledge of him, and from what relatives have said, he was a peculiar man, and my grandmother left him several times and took the children with her."

"However," said the old lady, rising. "Do come and have tea with me at Myrtle Cottage. It gets so lonely at times. I'd be so pleased . . ."

Had Derek told his aunt what he had seen she'd certainly have refused to let him out of her sight—if she didn't think he had become mentally deranged. That wouldn't solve anything, and it would only mean that his freedom might be curtailed, so he said nothing about the ghostly red eyes.

Later that day Derek met John Biddle.

"I say, Derek, don't say anything about that sack o' mine yesterday, will you?"

"No, of course not!"

"You see, a man has to feed his family as best he can . . ."

"I understand, Mr. Biddle."

"Call me John, lad. Now, tell me, what did you think of our ghostly mansion?"

Derek nodded. "Ghostly is right! I saw something weird, John."

Biddle's eyes gleamed with interest. "What did you see?"

"Well, it's hard to describe. It looked like two red eyes floating about in the air. They were there for only a short time before they disappeared."

"So . . .! I always knew there was something!"

"Have you seen anything?" asked Derek eagerly.

"At times I've imagined there was a shape, but nothing substantial. 'Tany rate, it's better not to dwell on such things, Derek. There's a thoroughly nasty feelin' about the place. Wouldn't be no bad thing if somebody bulldozed it flat."

"But the owner, Mrs. Terence, says they could never get workmen to stay any length of time there."

"Well, that's not our problem, me lad! We don't have to worry about that . . ."

"It seems a pity, though . . ."

"Well, I'd best be gettin' back to Station Road, or the wife'll put my dinner in the dustbin."

The following afternoon Derek was made to comb his hair, wash his face and put on a suit for tea at Myrtle Cottage. It was a tiny place, crammed to the picture rails with Mrs. Terence's collection of miniature paintings.

"I'd hate to have to sell any of these, but in last spring's gales some tiles became loosened, and something will have to be done about it."

What space on the walls and on top of the furniture was not occupied by miniatures, was filled with photographs of the family.

"And that," said Mrs. Terence, indicating a full-length,

66

yellowish studio portrait, "is bad old Grandfather Broadfoot himself."

Derek examined the protruding fierce eyes and the rat-trap mouth over the black beard.

"They do say that the awful man dabbled in things he oughtn't to," Mrs. Terence said, sensing Derek's interest. "Rumour even had it that he had a familiar."

"A familiar?" queried Derek, puzzled.

"Yes, a close companion. Usually it is an animal, a cat generally. People who have familiars are supposed to be able to change places with them, or be able to read their minds."

"Was it a cat your grandfather had?"

"Nobody knew what it was, so the story goes."

Aunt Greta gave a mock shudder. "Good heavens! How ghoulish you two have become!"

"Well, you know how legends grow up about odd people," said Mrs. Terence, laughing. "People just love making up stories about them."

Derek wished the old lady would go on talking about her grandfather, but guessed that she didn't want to say more in case it would upset Aunt Greta.

However, an opportunity arose later when the latter was out of the room.

"What kind of things did your grandfather dabble in?" asked Derek.

"Well, nobody ever really found out, but he had a large collection of books on magic and the occult, and whatever he did, he did behind closed doors."

She got up, opened a small cupboard and brought out a polished wooden casket. "Grandfather Broadfoot's ashes!" she whispered. "I don't know why I bother to keep them, except that I don't know quite what to do with them."

"Bury them in the grounds of Tockley House," suggested Derek. "I'll do it for you, if you like."

"What a good idea! Come and see me later and we'll talk about it."

Aunt Greta's entrance halted any further discussion.

Well, it was all very well for Derek to be brave and say that he'd go to Tockley House, dig a hole, and deposit in it Grandfather Broadfoot's only remains. But what about the eyes? And the hail of stones? It's all very well being brave when you know what you are up against. Whatever it was that was haunting Tockley House was a very unknown quantity indeed.

Then he thought of John Biddle.

It wasn't too difficult to track down the house in Station Road. The door was opened by a short, plump woman with a cheerful face and slightly greying hair.

"Yes, of course, my dear. Come in. He's in the back garden . . ."

The thatcher was momentarily surprised to see Derek, but got on with his digging while the boy explained why he was there.

"That, my lad," said John. "Might be dangerous."

"I know, John. That's why I can't do it alone and came to see you. Mr. Broadfoot was a weird old man. The odd things that have gone on there might have something to do with him. Taking his ashes there, well . . ."

"Hmmm." Biddle was silent for a long time. Then: "Well, I'll try anything once, I suppose. Never ever dug a grave afore!"

"When, John?"

"Any time you like, lad, so long as it's not after dark."

"Tomorrow morning?"

"Fair enough!"

Derek collected the casket from Mrs. Terence and met the thatcher standing waiting at his front gate with a spade and two bicycles. "We might want to get back down that road quicker'n we came."

He'd also brought two pieces of wood which he said they could use as shields if the stones started to fly.

It was a pleasant sunny morning, but the sky seemed to darken when they came in sight of the house. Derek couldn't understand how he'd ever thought that it looked harmless.

"Where shall we bury the casket, John?" he asked.

"Well," said Biddle, reaching to the heart of the matter. "If we're supposed to be tryin' to exorcise this ghost or whatever, I think the hole should be dug as near to the house as possible."

"All right." Derek's mouth felt dry with fear as he started to push his bike forward.

They walked slowly and warily, watching the open spaces and blank windows for any sign of movement.

"I just hope that what we're goin' to do won't bring up the fiends of hell around' us," whispered John hoarsely.

Twenty yards, ten yards . . . They'd passed the fountain. When the first missile thudded to the ground they were startled, in spite of knowing that it would happen.

John unstrapped the pieces of wood, and they edged forward towards the front steps under the bombardment that rattled and thudded on the wood.

"Right here, in front of the steps." gasped the thatcher. "Can't get any nearer without goin' inside! Hold the wood over me while I dig the hole."

Derek's unprotected knuckles and their legs took most of the onslaught.

"Won't be long now," grunted John breathlessly. "Reckon a couple of feet should be enough."

Derek realised that the fusillade of stones was ceasing and looked around. His heart almost stopped. Crouching on top of the steps behind John Biddle was a thing. Derek couldn't shout a warning because his mouth and throat were too dry.

It was pale—a pale green—and its skin was pitted and deeply lined. The arms were short and thin and the hands clawlike. The long legs resembled a frog's. Its pointed ears twitched and two long fangs covered the lower lip. Its eyes were malevolent slits of coral.

The thatcher looked up when Derek's nerveless hands dropped their wooden shelters, and his eyes followed those of the boy's.

"Gawd!" whispered Biddle. "What is it?"

The ears flattened as the man dropped the spade and its eyes blazed with fire.

How long they stood they could never afterwards hazard a guess. Derek had the horrible sensation that they might stand there for ever . . .

Slowly, slowly, John Biddle let his knees sag until he could reach the ground. The thing watched him, claws unsheathing.

"Careful, John!" begged Derek.

Keeping his eyes on the apparition, the man fumbled with the catch on the casket and flicked it open; then he pushed it towards the steps.

Finally, picking up the spade he pushed the casket closer still, until it was only a few feet from the steps.

The creature looked down. There was a sudden flare of red light from its eyes and, like a drift of smoke, something rose from the ashes inside the casket and took a vague shape. It appeared to be a tall figure—a man, a man with a beard—but later they could not be absolutely sure what they had seen.

Before the cloud of vapour enveloped the creature it emitted a squeal of delight and the ground seemed to shake with its purring.

Then, in a crack of lightning-like, blinding brilliance, the creature and the man disappeared.

When Derek and John examined the casket they found that it was empty.

"Let's put it in the hole, anyway," said John.

"D'you think that it was waiting all these years for Allan Broadfoot to come back?" asked the boy, awed.

"Could be."

"I wonder where they've gone . . ."

Biddle lit his pipe, sighed and wiped the sweat of fright from his forehead. "Well, one thing's for sure—it won't be heaven, will it, lad?"

From that day the ruins and grounds of Tockley House were left undisturbed. Derek learned later that the farmer whose land abutted gave Mrs. Terence a good price for it.

Only John and Derek knew about the reunion of Broadfoot and his familiar. As Biddle said: "What's the point in talking about it? Nobody would believe us, anyway."

THE HANGING TREE

by SYDNEY J. BOUNDS

"THERE'S the turn-off," said Roy Jackson excitedly, pointing to a road sign and its painted legend:

TOMBSTONE GULCH

His father slowed the car and turned off the main highway on to a stony track leading deep into the Arizona desert. "Don't expect too much, Roy. It's only a ghost town now." He wiped sweat from his face. "I must say it's a relief to be able to take it easy again. These American highways are a bit nerve-racking."

The late afternoon sun was bright and hot, and dust rose in a grey cloud as they bumped and rattled through the scrub. They seemed to be alone in the world—a startling contrast after the high-speed traffic on the highway.

Roy said confidently: "Now we'll see the West as it really is."

"It could be pretty dull," his father warned. "Nobody lives here any more."

Mr. Jackson was visiting the United States on business and had brought Roy with him as a special treat. Roy was fourteen and a Western buff, and his father had promised that they would stop off at a ghost town—one of the old Western settlements that had died as America progressed into the space age.

They didn't see a single human being on the forty-mile drive through desert country. It was a desolate area where only cacti grew. Presently they crested a hill and saw Tombstone Gulch below.

"Like something out of a film," Mr. Jackson chuckled. "Just one wide street with wooden shacks on each side."

A single tree grew all alone at the near end of town where Main Street began; an old tree, straight and strong, with a thick, almost-horizontal branch jutting out at right-angles.

"At least it casts a bit of shade," Mr. Jackson said. "We'll camp here I think."

He drove under the tree and stopped. They got out of the car and stretched. The sun was low, filling the length of Main Street with golden light and shadow.

Roy tugged at his father's arm. "Come on, let's explore."

Mr. Jackson smiled. "All right, a bit of exercise won't hurt, though I don't expect there's much to see. One thing, don't go into any of the buildings—they're old and likely to collapse."

Together they set off down the wide dusty street of the old Western town. Their footprints followed them in the dust.

"Certainly proves nobody's been here for a long time, Roy."

They walked past saloons with batwing doors and broken windows and faded names like *Last Chance* and *Silver Dollar*. Next to the Wells Fargo office was the blacksmith's shop. There was a general store and two hotels and a bank. Further on, the sheriff's office and jail. At the far end of town was the broken fence of a horse corral. The whole town was deserted and eerie with the wind stirring the dust and setting old boards creaking.

"It's creepy," Roy said. "No wonder they call it a ghost town!"

They walked back along the empty street, their footsteps the only sound.

"It really is like a film set, isn't it, Dad? I wonder what it was like years ago."

Mr. Jackson laughed. "Dirty and smelly, I should think!"

They reached their car parked under the lone tree and made a meal of hamburgers and beans over a portable stove. Dusk settled over Tombstone Gulch, the sagging wooden shacks silhouetted against the blood red of a setting sun.

While Mr. Jackson erected their tent, Roy shinned up the tree and sprawled out along the branch, looking down the length of Main Street.

He was startled to see a light come on in one of the saloons. The warm yellow of an oil lamp. A piano tinkled a melody. Other lights came on as darkness crept over the town. Roy stared in fascination as a group of cowboys rode in from the far end, dismounted and hitched their horses to the rail along the boardwalk. Spurs jangled as they pushed through the batwings.

He saw the glow of cigarettes as men sat on benches. A door banged and a voice sang quietly:

"Oh, Susannah! Don't you cry for me,

For I'm off to California . . ."

Hoofs clip-clopped into town. Roy saw a lone rider on a big horse; he was dressed all in black with a flat-crowned hat and a Colt .45 holstered on his left side.

Talk died away as the rider dismounted outside the *Last Chance*. The street began to clear. A batwing door swung open and a youth in cowboy garb came out to face the newcomer; he was not much older than Roy, but his manner was aggressive and he, too, was armed.

"I hear tell you're fast with a gun, Blackie," the youth said. "I reckon you'll have to prove it—or get out of town!"

As the challenge echoed down Main Street, Blackie backed away, keeping his gaze fixed on the youth. They faced each other, alone in the wide expanse of dust.

Blackie's draw was too fast for Roy to see. He had a gun in his hand and a red flame stabbed out. A single shot reverberated and the youth keeled over and lay sprawled on the ground, the front of his shirt stained.

Blackie stood motionless as a man ran out and crouched over the youth's body. "Dead," he pronounced in a ringing tone.

Roy felt the chill of horror. He had seen a man killed and that was no longer amusing. This was not a film, this was truly happening. He felt cold, cold as a grave. His limbs were paralyzed.

A crowd gathered, silently ringing the gunman. There were too many of them for him to shoot his way out and he holstered his gun and faced them calmly. "The kid

Roy saw a lone rider . . .

challenged me," he stated. "He didn't leave me any get-out."

"There was no need to kill him, Blackie. It would have been enough to have winged him."

The crowd pressed closer round the gunman, roughing him up. His hat was knocked off to reveal a shock of white hair. A burly man with a star pinned to his shirt forced a way through the crowd.

"All right," he said. "Leave him to me now."

Blackie's gun was taken from him and he was hustled down the street towards the jail.

As the figures faded into shadow beyond the oil-lamps, Roy felt his paralysis broken. Hurriedly he slid down the tree-trunk.

His father said: "Time for bed, Roy," and then saw how white his son's face was. "Are you all right?"

Roy turned to stare down the dark and gloomy length of Main Street. "Didn't you see——?"

"See what, Roy? There's nothing to see."

"Didn't you hear anything?"

"Only the wind blowing."

Roy said, "There was a gunfight. I saw——" He broke off, not sure that he'd really seen anything.

Mr. Jackson looked curiously at him. "It must be your imagination. There's nothing to see or hear—it's a ghost town."

"Ghost!" Roy echoed, and shivered as though the night had turned cold.

"Just try to forget whatever you think you saw," his father said. "Go to bed now. We'll be away from here in the morning."

Roy crawled into his sleeping bag, but sleep did not come easily. For a long time, his mind dwelt on the youth he had seen shot down. But, finally, he fell asleep.

He was wakened by a hand shaking him gently. He started up in a sweat, suddenly afraid. But it was his father shaking him and saying in a cheerful voice. "Breakfast's ready—come and get it."

Outside the tent, the dawn sun cast a pale light over Tombstone Gulch. He tried to eat the fried sausages—one of his favourite meals—but they tasted like sawdust.

The deserted town stayed silent. Only the wind stirred. Had he really seen anything last night . . .? He knew, deep down, that he had.

Mr. Jackson started to take down the tent and pack their sleeping bags in the car.

Roy stared towards the town. It seemed a different place now, a place to fear. Overhead, a buzzard spiralled.

Roy felt curiosity. Why had only he seen it? And why only from the tree? His pulse quickened . . . it had to be the tree. The tree had been there when it happened, years ago . . .

Curious, afraid of what he might see, yet unable to resist a last look, he shinned up the tree and lay flat on the branch. And the town came to life in the dawn light.

A party of men walked the length of Main Street in a compact group. They were grim-faced and silent. In their centre walked Blackie, his white head bare; Roy saw that his hands were tied.

They came silently towards the lone tree, towards Roy . . . could they see him on the branch? Again he knew the grip of fear. Ice-cold sweat formed on his body.

The posse reached the tree. The sheriff carried a coiled rope. As he uncoiled it, he looked up at the branch, and his gaze appeared to meet Roy's. Then Roy saw the noose in the end of the rope and knew what came next . . .

As the sheriff cast the rope upward over the branch, Roy slid down the trunk in a panic. When he reached the bottom, the posse vanished as though it had never existed.

He was alone except for his father, calling from the car. "See anything up there?"

Roy shook his head. He was too scared to speak. He got in the car and his father started up and drove away from Tombstone Gulch.

Roy looked back briefly and it seemed to him that he saw a dark shape hanging from the branch. He shuddered, blinking his eyes, and in that moment the image vanished.

THE OLD MAN OF THE HILLS

by MARY CLARKE

JIMMY CHOW almost turned and ran away when he saw Mr. Watson, the schoolmaster, stop at the cemetery gates.

All the week he had looked forward to the nature-study expedition up to Tormore Crag, but it had never crossed his mind that they might go by way of the short cut through the broken-down old graveyard.

Mr. Watson pushed open the creaking gate.

"Come along, boys!" he shouted. "Don't dawdle. We've a long way to go."

Like a pioneer thrusting through the jungle he led the way, thrashing down with his walking stick the creeping vegetation which threatened to close the narrow paths.

The boys, thirty or so of them, followed. Most of them clowned as they went, but Jimmy walked quietly, his eyes looking straight ahead.

He hated the place. Drunken angels leaned lopsidedly from sunken gravestones, beckoning with broken fingers, and rotting mausoleum doors moved in the wind. In the darkness of the catacombs, fern fronds dipped and waved from their foothold in dank, damp, stone walls.

With ghost-like touch an elongated leaf brushed Jimmy's cheek to send a shock of horror down his spine.

He gasped and edged his way between two of his chums so that they flanked him on either side, keeping him from contact with those people of the past. There, he felt safer.

But suddenly he was grabbed from behind and tugged towards one of those terrifying gaping doors.

"In you go, Chow the Chinaman. Go where you belong."

Jimmy screamed and, twisting himself free, saw that his tormentor was Race, a thick-set older boy who delighted in tormenting him whenever he got the chance.

"I hate you, Race!" Jimmy yelled. He was wiry though small, and he clenched his fists ready to punch if Race grabbed him again. But Race doubled up, his arms clasped tightly about himself as if howling with laughter.

Pattinson, the sixth-former on the expedition with them, came over.

"Stop pestering Chow," he commanded Race, and he yanked the bigger boy across the path. "What's wrong with you anyway? You look even more horrible than usual."

"Chow stuck something into me," Race gasped. His face was pasty-white and he bit his lips in pain.

"Did you, Chow?" Pattinson asked.

"I didn't touch him. He grabbed me," Jimmy said indignantly, and the others joined in, agreeing with him.

"I expect you've got a stitch," Pattinson said with little sympathy. "Now come on, get a move on. We're dropping behind the rest."

Mr. Watson had stopped and was looking back.

"If you're making trouble again, Race, I'll send you

back to the school," he called out. "We can't delay, there's a long climb ahead and lots of work to do."

It was warm once they got out on to the hill, and they climbed higher than they had ever gone before so that they could study the effects of height and stronger winds on plant life.

After a while they divided into two groups, one with Mr. Watson and one with Pattinson. Jimmy was in the latter group—and so too was Race, but Jimmy kept well away from him.

Shouts of laughter could be heard as the boys scrambled over boulders, and cries of triumph when they made some exciting discovery.

Jimmy found a sundew on the edge of a boggy piece of ground and Pattinson explained how the small plant closed around any insect which dared to alight upon it and held it tight until the breath of life was squeezed from its body.

"You did well to find that, Chow," he praised Jimmy. "There are not many of them in these parts."

"There might be another one," Jimmy said, and he darted off into a hollow surrounded by boulders. Stooping down, he hunted around as the sun beat warmly on his shoulders.

But, suddenly, something blotted out the sun and a huge menacing shadow, like a giant gorilla with arms raised and ready to leap, fell on the rock before him.

His heart beat fast as if it was going to burst from his body until, at last, he slowly dared to turn his head to see what monster threatened.

The ugly, sneering face of Race loomed above him. Jimmy scrambled away, but Race was on him and threw him to the ground, lying on top of him, his hands round his throat.

"So, Chow the Chinaman's the clever one, is he?" he snarled. "Chow found a sundew! Look what I've found, teacher!" he mimicked.

Jimmy flinched. "Leave me alone, Race. I've never done anything to you."

Race knelt back on his heels. "O.K., Chow, I'm not going to do anything to you."

A shuddering sigh of relief shook Jimmy.

Race patted his face lightly. "You're glad, are you, Jimmy? I'm bigger than you. I could hurt you a lot, couldn't I, Jimmy?" He smiled a sneaky, sinister smile. "I'm not going to hurt you—not now. But this evening when we go back . . ."

He kept on smiling that dreadful smile, and Jimmy gulped.

"When we go back," Race drawled on, "through the cemetery, through the catacombs, I'm going to keep you back behind the rest, then I'm going to *pop*——" He held his hands high and clenched them. "I'm going to *pop* you into one of those tombs, and I'm going to shut the door."

He put his sallow, pimply face near to Jimmy's.

"That tomb will be like a sundew. It will close round you, and—if you tell anyone what I've said—it will *never* let you go."

He got up. " 'Bye for now," he said casually and lumbered clumsily away.

Jimmy lay there shaking. He was so terrified he felt sick. There was only one thing for it. Somehow he had to escape. Somehow he'd got to get back home on his own so that he didn't have to go through that terrible graveyard again.

He went back to the group and spoke to Pattinson.

"I'm going to show the sundew to Mr. Watson," he said

81

and he pointed in the direction of the voices coming from a dip in the hill.

"Do that, Jimmy," Pattinson said. "He will be delighted you have found one."

Jimmy went off but, directly he was out of view, he dropped down into the gully between some high rocks and slithered down on to a track well away from the route the two groups would take on their way home. He wouldn't be missed because on such trips they dispersed when they got to the town, and Pattinson would think he had got back with Mr. Watson, while Mr. Watson would, of course, assume he was still with Pattinson.

Going the long way round would make him later home, but he had some money and once on the road he could get a bus.

Thankful to be away from Race, he hurried along in the sunshine until, like a bolt from the blue, an avalanche of small rocks rumbled down from higher up the hill.

Jimmy froze in his tracks, petrified in the belief that Race was somewhere up there above him, ready to pounce from a rocky hiding place. He was worse off than ever now, for there was no one within call.

But an eerie silence followed and Jimmy, his eyes sliding from left to right, watching for the enemy he was sure must be there, rushed down the hill, his feet scarcely touching the ground, as if Satan himself were after him.

His toes caught on a projecting tree root and down he fell, his body spinning over and over, going down, into endless space until a rocky ledge caught and held him.

When he came to, the sun was low and the wind was cold. Bewildered, he sat up and, as memory returned, he gingerly fingered his aching head. He shook first one arm and then the other. They worked fine. His legs, too. They ached but, still, they weren't broken.

Cautiously he lowered himself down from the ledge on to the grassy slope but, when he started to walk, his left ankle gave beneath his full weight and he sprawled to the ground.

Loneliness and the awfulness of his plight swept over him and tears crept down his face. No one would pass that way at that time. Neither Mr. Watson nor Pattinson would miss him, and his mother would start to worry when he didn't get home to the Chinese restaurant his father ran.

When he thought of his mother, he sobbed aloud.

Then he heard a voice saying, very kindly: "Don't cry, child."

It was so extraordinary, so unexpected, that Jimmy thought he had imagined it. It wasn't just that he was surprised to hear a voice, this voice had spoken in Chinese!

"Pu yao k'u, hai-tzi," it had said. Jimmy didn't know of any other Chinese people in the district, apart from his own family—just his father, mother, and himself. But he did understand Chinese, although he had been born in England, because his parents spoke it between themselves and had taught him to speak it too, right from the time he was a baby. So he understood what the voice said perfectly.

The gentle voice came again: *"Ngo k'o-i pang-tsu ni,"* it said this time, which meant: I can help you.

Jimmy looked round to see where the voice came from. Sitting on his haunches not far off was an old, old Chinese man. Jimmy had never seen anyone like him before, except in the books on old China his mother showed him.

The old man was tall for a Chinese; he had a long, wispy beard and a grey pigtail—although the hair on the top of his head was sparse.

He wore a coarse blue cotton gown with a girdle tied

83

round the waist. The gown was split up the sides to the hips and underneath was a pair of baggy blue cotton trousers.

The old man got up. "Come on, lad," he said.

The arm he put around Jimmy to support him was wafer-thin, and a puff of wind would have blown away the body against which Jimmy leaned. But it had, nevertheless, a timeless resilience about it, and the cold wind, the rocks, the slippery slope and the darkness presented no difficulties to Jimmy's new friend.

They reached the main road safely and stood by the bus stop.

"Thank you, sir," Jimmy said. "You have been very kind. I can get a bus from here which will take me right home." He spoke in Chinese.

"Bus." The old man repeated the word and giggled at the explosive sound of the Chinese as if it was something he had never heard before.

Jimmy laughed too, because the old man exaggerated the sound and made it like an engine back-firing. He was nice, he thought, and his mother would like to meet him.

"Where do you live, sir?" he asked.

"Live? Where do I live?" He laughed as if it was a great joke. "Live? Ha-ha! I've got to go. *Tsai-chien* (Goodbye)."

Jimmy hobbled on to the bus when it came and, hanging on to the rail, he turned to wave to his friend, but the old man had already disappeared.

Jimmy lay in bed, his ankle comfortably bound up by his mother. His injury had been the excuse for his lateness, and he had said nothing about Race's behaviour, his terror of the cemetery, or the way he had separated from the rest of the party.

He was going to tell of his meeting with the old man

but, when he was about to start on the story, something seemed to stop him, as if the man had whispered in his ear: "That's between you and me, lad."

So he said nothing.

His head rested on the pillows. He was safe and happy at home. His dark eyes smiled up at his mother sitting beside the bed. She smiled back at him and stroked the lock of black hair up off his forehead.

She was very pretty, he thought. Her hair shone and she coiled it in a heap on top of her head. She wore a lovely sea-green silk Chinese gown with a high collar, and she was very slim.

"Tell me a story, Mummy," he urged. That was how he always liked to end the day—learning a bit more about their native land. She told him of the old home where all the family had lived together, the great rivers, the floods, the famines, the temples, and the way the rice grew in the paddy fields.

She held his hand. "I think tonight," she said, speaking slowly in Chinese, "I'll tell you a Chinese legend—one you will never find printed in a book, I fear. In a way, it's a cautionary tale, telling us not to reach out for the impossible. Now this legend is about . . ."

The way she said it in a drawly, husky voice tantalised him with a mixture of delight and a pleasant sort of fear. Some of the fairy stories she told were really eerie—but he loved them.

She turned off the ceiling light and the room, lit by the small bedside lamp, was dim. Her shadow fell lightly on the wall. Hissing, spitting noises snapped their way upwards from the restaurant below as moist shredded meat was tossed into hot fat.

". . . about an old man," Mrs. Chow went on dreamily. "This old man, so foolish really, but very, very dear."

She paused and peeped over her shoulder. "He seems

so near tonight," she whispered. Her voice brightened and she said spontaneously: "I love him, I really love this old man."

Jimmy snuggled down into the bedclothes. He, too, had a strange feeling of a presence there—a good presence.

"Go on," he urged breathlessly.

"The old man of the hills," she drawled as if half asleep. Then she went on more quickly: "He was tall and slight and he had a pigtail and a beard."

"But he was almost bald on top," Jimmy broke in.

Mrs. Chow laughed softly. "Now how did you guess that?" she asked. "He always wore coarse blue cotton clothes, a long gown with baggy trousers underneath and a girdle round the waist."

"What was the girdle for?" Jimmy had been dying to ask the old man that but was afraid of seeming rude.

"He had a girdle because he was a great walker and the long gown was a hindrance. So he used to tuck the front skirt of his split gown up into the girdle. Like that he was able to stride out more easily."

"Where did he want to walk to?" Jimmy asked.

"Now don't keep interrupting," she chided him gently. "He had a great ambition, just one thing he wanted to do in his remaining years. He wanted to walk to the horizon."

"Oh!" Jimmy gasped, and then covered his lips with his hands as his mother's look admonished him not to interrupt again.

"He started off," she went on, "with a stout blackthorn stick carved with a Buddha's head. The horizon, so he said, was only at the top of the mountains which lay to the south of his village. He reasoned it would take him about three days to get there. So he packed a bag with food and off he went."

Jimmy's eyes were fixed upon her moving lips as if he could see the words coming out.

"Exactly in three days he reached the top of the mountains but . . ." She paused. "The . . . horizon . . . was . . . not . . . there. It was on top of another range of mountains much further south."

Jimmy could sense deep inside himself the terrible disappointment of the traveller. An old man, weary, keyed up by hope, and then at the end to find it all a sort of mirage.

Mrs. Chow went on: "However, the old man had great determination. He rested and then continued towards the horizon. He went on for years . . . and years . . . and years. But the horizon never got any nearer. It was always ahead, always out of reach." Her voice was low and solemn. "At last, he could endure no more."

Her tempo changed and the words came tumbling out: "A great anger tore him and, in a mighty rage, he threw the blackthorn to the ground . . ." Her hands were clasped tightly and her face flushed. "The old man stood there looking at his lovely stick and—even as he looked—it turned into a rearing, spitting viper. The old man stepped back in terror. The snake's head darted forward, its tongue curled out. It weaved and dipped. It played with the old man's fear . . . It came so far, then drew back that hideous head."

She spoke in a whisper. "It took one last thrust, its tongue a hair's breadth from the old man's face. It quivered there, hypnotising, holding the man to the spot. It was too much for him. He fell to the ground. He was dead. He had died of fright—so very far from home."

There was quietness in the room. Tears smarted at Jimmy's closed eyelids. At last he asked:

"How far did he get?"

"I don't know, darling."

"Do you think he got as far as England?" he asked.

She laughed softly. "I shouldn't think so."

"He could have done," Jimmy ventured. "Chinese junks sailed the seas many, many years ago."

"They did indeed," she agreed. "Perhaps," she said jokingly, "the old man of the hills is the unknown Chinese buried in the old cemetery here."

Jimmy stared. "You never told me," he said accusingly.

"It happened a very, very long time ago," she said. "The story is told around here that a Chinese man was found dead on Tormore Crag. It was thought he must have been a seaman on leave from a ship and that he was walking across country to get somewhere.

"People were moved by the thought of a stranger dying so far from home, so a lovely tomb was built for him by public subscription. It's broken down now and the door is hanging off its hinges. But I've been told that the inscription can still be seen."

"What does it say?" Jimmy asked.

"Rest in Peace, Chinese stranger in our midst."

"He's happy here," Jimmy said thoughtfully.

"What a funny thing to say," she laughed. "Sleep well."

"Good-night, Mummy." After she had gone, he said aloud in the empty room: "Good-night, sir, and thank you for helping me. One day I'll try to get your tomb repaired."

A thought struck him.

"Race knew that tomb was yours. He must have. That's why he said I belonged there."

He chuckled. "But he didn't reckon you'd still be around to give him a dig in the ribs!"

THE FUN FAIR GHOST

by RAY GOTTLIEB

THE Fun Fair opened up in May and stayed the whole summer. I hung around there a lot. It was pretty dead all the week, but on Saturday nights it was really swinging, and you could hear the noise for miles around. I loved the lights and the music, and the sideshows, and the people and the candyfloss and the smell. It was like everyone was happy and enjoying themselves and shouting and laughing. The roller coaster was the best. Whee-ee-ee, up we went, and Whoosh!—straight down, like a dive bomber. Trouble was, I never had enough money. Only 50p a week Mum gave me.

"Quite enough for a boy of twelve," she says. "When I was your age I only had sixpence a week."

Then she gives me a pep talk about how she never kept on nagging *her* Mum, but was always so grateful and all that.

"But, Mum," I says. "Mu-um . . ."

"No!" she says. "No! And that's final. Now, get out from under my feet. Sit down and watch the telly, and let me get my hair done. I'll be late for Bingo."

Dad just sits there, doing his Pools most of the time, or reading the Sports page, or watching the telly.

"Do as your Mum says, you little blighter," he says, but he never really interferes. In our house it's what Mum says that goes.

Well, one Saturday morning, she's gone round to the supermarket and he's sitting there as usual, so I go off to see how things are doing at the Fair. They haven't opened up properly yet, and sitting on a chair outside the Ghost Train there's this big, fat geezer, who runs the show. The Ghost Train is really great. There's a tunnel, all dark, and a little train without a top, and weird noises, and then suddenly there's a flash of light and a skeleton jumps out at you, rattling its bones. Then a bat flies over your head, and all kinds of scary things like that, and you can hear the birds screaming and the fellers laughing.

So this chap sees me standing there, and he looks at me with his sharp little eyes, very twinkly they are, and he says:

"Come here, son. How would you like to earn some money?"

So I says to him, "What sort of money? Doing what?"

So he says, "I need someone to help out every Saturday with the effects."

What's effects? I think to myself, but I say nothing and just look alert and intelligent—I hope.

"Saturdays we like to put on a really good show," he says. "People nowadays want kicks. I need a kid, who won't take up too much room, to hide in the tunnel and touch a few people as the train goes past. The ghostly hand, and all that. Just tickle them gently. Every Saturday, from eight till eleven. A quid. How about it?".

This sounds like a real giggle. I wouldn't have minded doing it for nothing, but getting paid for a job like that sounds a bit of all right.

"O.K.," I says. "I can start this evening, if you like."

I know that *they* don't start to get the needle unless I'm out later than twelve.

Then he shows me the inside of the tunnel. It's pretty black at first, but after you've been there a little while your eyes get used to the dark, and you can just about see what's going on. There was a little space behind a post where I could hide. I had to wear a black cloak with a hood that fell over my face, with slits for my eyes and mouth, so that I would be invisible to anyone coming in from the bright lights outside.

Things started a bit slow at eight o'clock, but by nine it was really crowded, and the train was nearly full on every run. I soon got the hang of it, and found out it was best to touch a bird on the back of the neck, or just grip her shoulder for a second. That made them scream the loudest, and, of course, the louder they screamed the better it was for business, because then the people outside wanted to have a go and find out for themselves what it was all about. And some of those birds sounded like a police siren gone mad, I promise you.

I could see the fat geezer was pleased when he handed over the quid at eleven o'clock.

"See you next week, son," he said.

"Sure, Dad," I said, kind of offhand—never let them take you for granted—but I was pretty pleased with myself, too.

Next week I turn up at eight o'clock, all set to go, but this time it isn't such a good night for business, as it's raining, so, of course, there aren't too many people around. There are some fairly long waits between trips, so I just sit there, waiting for the train to come through, and thinking about what I'm going to spend my money on.

Everything has been nice and peaceful for about fifteen minutes or so, when suddenly I hear someone sighing very close to my ear, and like a chain rattling. The train's not running, so where are the sounds coming from? At first I think it's someone messing about with the equipment. Then there's a noise like teeth chattering, and someone gives a horrible moan and gasp, as if they're suffering dreadful tortures like you see on the telly. I stare very hard into the dark, and I can make out some sort of a figure next to me. I can just catch a glimpse of something floating in the air in the shape of a body. I am quite sure it isn't one of the effects, I can somehow feel that it's operating off its own steam, so to speak. So I sit there and wait, and the thing stays there, like it's waiting as well. Then I hear a voice which seems to come from somewhere near the top of it.

"What manner of spirit art thou, sirrah?" it says, in a very posh voice, which sounds kind of far away, even though it's also right next to my ear-hole. "Why dost thou haunt this spot, which," it says, "was apportioned to me but yesterday, for my sole use and enjoyment, at our conventicle"—or did he say convention?—"in the dungeons of the Tower of London. Not," it adds, kind of bitter, "that this is a fitting office for one of my high and mighty estate—I, who, in my time, have struck terror into the hearts of the stoutest mortals, and chilled the very blood in their veins till it ceased to flow. But times are hard, and I must needs accept even this lowly charge. So, froward youth, be off! Let me see thee no more. Avaunt! Depart!"

And it lets out what it thinks is a blood-curdling wail. Of course, the poor so-and-so doesn't know that I'm used to hearing my mum when she really lets go, and his effort doesn't amount to much compared with her. So I just stay put, very suave, real cool—only I don't bother to put on my James Bond expression, as I figure it will probably be wasted because of the hood which I'm wearing—and I say:

"So what, mate? I was here first. This is my pitch, and I'm not giving it up, so don't try to give me all that creepy stuff. Depart thyself!" I says, having a bash at the olde-tyme chat myself, "and let me get on with the job."

By straining my eyes very hard, I could begin to make out a bit more. I could see one of those Elizabethan ruffs, and I think there was a little pointy beard. I could see through him to the opposite wall of the tunnel. It was like looking through a window all covered with dust. The face wasn't clear, but every time he spoke there were like little points of light glittering from his eyes, or the holes where they used to be. Then there was a noise like it sucked in its breath, and little flashes of light began to flicker all round its edges.

"Have a care, lest my wrath be not provoked against thee," it hissed. "Thy tender years shall not save thee. Defy me not, but take thy leave forthwith."

Well, everyone knows that ghosts go straight through things, without being able to touch them, so I think to my self, let him moan as much as he likes, he can't really do anything to me.

Then suddenly I feel a very hard pinch on my arm, and I nearly hit the roof with the shock of it.

"Here, hold on a minute!" I shouted. "I thought ghosts were supposed to go through everything, so how can you make yourself felt?"

There was this little flash from his eyes again, and he said :

"A simple device, fellow, perfected by one of the Counsellors but lately admitted to our company. Suffice it to say that I am now able to make physical contact at will."

"How come?" I said.

"Electronically controlled impulses," he said, and he rolled the words round his tongue like they were some fantastic magic spell or something.

Then he laughed horribly, and rattled his chains a bit, just to keep in practice, I suppose.

I do a bit of quick thinking. Then I says, "Well, in that case, why don't we talk things over?" I nearly said man to man, but I figured that might sound a bit too corny, even for him.

He laughed horribly . . .

"Look," I said, "I was here first, and you know that gives me the right to stay." I tried to sound like I stood for justice and fair play and all that. "But I'll go away and leave you in peace, on one condition."

"Name it," he says.

"Well, it's like this," I says. "There's this train, see?"

"Train?" he says, kind of puzzled.

"Well, look," I says. "Just watch me, and you'll soon catch on. Hold tight, here it comes now."

And, as it rattles past, I go into the old routine, real artistic, and give him a demonstration.

"Now," I says, "that's all you've got to do. But there's one thing you've got to swear, on your honour as a ghost, or whatever you do swear by. Pinch them gently. Don't overdo it."

His eyes flickered like mad, and he laughed.

"By my troth, fine sport indeed," says he. Then he goes all solemn, and recites in a very deep voice:

"By the power of the foe who betrayed me, by the block and the axe which despatched me, by the shade of the darkness which binds me, I swear."

"Then it's all yours, mate," I said, and I very quietly crept out of the tunnel through the back, where the geezer in charge couldn't see me. As I left, I heard the train coming through, and piercing shrieks, and lots of giggling and laughing, so I knew everything was O.K.

The rain had stopped by then, the crowds were pouring in, and I had a marvellous time going round the Fair for the rest of the evening. All I had to do was keep out of the fat geezer's way, which wasn't difficult, as he sat in a sort of box affair and worked all the gadgets. Every now and again I came near enough to hear the goings-on in the Ghost Train. They didn't half make a row.

At eleven o'clock I turned up as if I had just walked out of the tunnel, and collected my money.

"See you next week, son," he said.

"Sure, Pop," I said.

This went on all the rest of the summer. Not bad, eh?

But I've been thinking. Next year I might try the tunnel of love. I mean, if the convention, or conventicle, or whatever they call themselves, are sending a ghost there as well, why, with any kind of luck, I could be all set to double my money.

THE CURSE OF THE WHITE OWL

by TIM VICARY

"THE woman never did her any harm. She just knew that, at any time, she might look up and see a ghostly face watching her. It was a kind face, she said, and she said that in the end she almost got to like it. But it never went away."

Sara shivered as she lay under the bedclothes. Her wide eyes stared at the black ceiling, but she saw nothing; she was still thinking of the girl in the story Simon had just told. Sara almost felt she was that girl. Only after a few minutes did she begin to relax. She saw the pale patterns the moonlight traced on the bookcase and the wardrobe as the wind lifted the curtain by the open window. Then the curtain fell back and the wall was black. Very faintly, she could hear her father playing the piano in his study that was supposed to be soundproofed.

At last she spoke. Her voice sounded strangely husky in the dark room.

"Do you believe it, Simon? It couldn't really be true, could it?"

"How should I know? She said it was true. I bet it was true, as well."

Sara didn't think that was very satisfactory. She didn't think Simon really believed the ghost story he had just told, but she couldn't be sure.

"Anyway, I'm going to sleep. Goodnight." She heard Simon turn over, rustling the sheets loudly for a moment as she settled down. Then silence. The curtain flapped softly again, and she heard the click of footsteps and mumble of voices from the road outside as some people walked home from the pub. An owl shrieked in the woods across the river. Sara turned over again restlessly. It was no good talking to Simon now. He would only tease her; she had heard that in the tone of his voice.

But as soon as she turned over, to face the wall, she had the uncomfortable feeling that there was a face behind her, watching, staring at the back of her head. Don't be silly, she thought, it's only the story—but when she closed her eyes all she could see was the face of the ghostly woman as she had imagined her, smiling sadly at the little girl. The back of her neck tingled. At last she could bear it no longer and turned, slowly but surely, forcing her eyes to stare straight into the place where the face would have been.

Nothing. Just the usual shadows; a glint from the mirror, the pale square of the window behind the curtain, the dark shape of the desk. And yet the shadows themselves seemed suspicious. She sighed and closed her eyes—but opened them at once to stare at the shadows again, as though only by staring at them could she keep them in place. There was something about them; and now she was sure there was someone watching her from behind, between her and the wall . . .

There was a soft thump from the foot of her bed. She sat upright, quickly, staring into the dark. Nothing, nothing

D

. . . then another thump, sharper than before. And another. Tap, tap. And a shape moved. It was the chair—the chair at the foot of her bed! Tap, tap. The sound again; and she saw the chair move with it—*the chair was moving towards her*!

Tap, tap. Sara sat bolt upright and screamed. "Aaaaaaah! Aaaaaaah! Simon, help! Aaaaaaah!"

The chair stopped. There was a funny, smothered, snuffling sound from the floor by her bed. It wasn't frightening; in fact, there was something oddly normal about it. Something very funny—and *very* annoying. It was Simon laughing helplessly.

"Simon! You little pig! You nasty smelly little rat!" She jumped out of bed to hit him, but he stumbled away, still laughing, to his own bed.

"You believed it! The chairs are coming to get you! Ha ha—ow!"

Sara grabbed a pillow and swiped clumsily at where she thought he was, but already his laughter was beginning to affect her as well. She had to laugh, even if she had looked silly. The ghostly chair was nothing, just the ordinary wooden one it had always been. Simon must have crept out of the far side of his bed when he had been pretending to go to sleep, and wormed his way slowly across the floor to the chair.

"And how you screamed!" he said. " 'Simon, help!' If there was a ghost in here you'd have burst its eardrums!"

"D'you reckon Dad heard?" They stopped for a moment and listened. But there was still the faint sound of piano music from the study, as though someone was playing the piano a long way away, over a lake.

"No," said Sara. "It's probably really loud in there. He wouldn't hear anything."

"We could be murdered in here and he would never know."

"Only when Mum's away, like tonight," said Sara. "Anyway, don't be daft! Who'd want to murder us, Simple Simon?"

"Who knows? They might be creeping up outside this house at this very moment. Hey, listen, what was . . .?" But Sara's second pillow knocked him on his back before he could say anything else. He threw one back, and there was a wild pillow-fight which reduced everything in the room to chaos. When they had finished, and scrambled some of the bedclothes back into heaps on their beds, they were too wide awake to sleep. So they lay and talked.

It was always like this with Simon. Sara hadn't been very pleased when she was told he was coming down from Birmingham to stay for a week, and she had been angry with him dozens of times since then. He was a town boy from a large family; she was a country girl used to spending time quietly on her own, and many of the things he did made her mad. He had thrown stones at the cows in the nearby field, making them gallop around crazily and nearly break the fence; he had let out the rabbits and set the cat among them just to see what would happen; he had insisted on playing football in the garden until half the flowerbeds were ruined; and he had been horribly rude to the vicar's wife when she had caught them cycling along the footpath by the churchyard.

And yet, despite all this, she quite liked him. After all, the vicar's wife *was* a fussy old baggage, although Sara would never have dared to say anything to her; and he had helped her to catch the rabbits when she had asked him. It was fun, too, to learn some of the bicycle riding tricks he had taught her; and he did know a lot of good stories. Sara had to admit that it was interesting having Simon to stay. The trouble was, he was always that little bit better at everything; and he was so full of what he wanted to do, that he had no time for the things that interested her when she was on her own. On her own, Sara spent hours growing flowers and strange weeds in her garden; or lying very still, listening to the trees whispering to each other; or wondering why the owls seemed to follow her in the evenings—but she knew these things would seem silly to Simon, so she never mentioned them. She wondering if he thought her dull. She was always trying to play his games, trying to keep up.

"I bet there are a few ghosts in this old village," said Simon, as they lay in their separate beds, talking. "Do you know of any?"

"No. No, not really. Not real ghosts."

An owl shrieked again outside the window, quite close this time. It sounded like Sara's scream.

"What was that, then?" said Simon.

"Just an owl," said Sara. "They often shriek round here."

"That was never an owl. They go tooo-wit, to-whooo, like this." Simon tried, unsuccessfully, to make a hoot by blowing into his fists.

"You're thinking of another sort of owl. These are barn owls. They just shriek. We might see it if we look out."

Sara got up and drew back the curtains, and they leaned out of the window. The house was a bungalow on a low hill, and they could see, beyond the shrubs in the garden, the lights of houses and the darker forms of trees in the village below. Quite near, the old church tower stood stark against the sky. For a long time they watched and saw nothing. Then a pale shape floated silently across from a yew tree, and up into a hole high in the church tower.

"That's where they nest," said Sara. "They'll be taking food home for their chicks."

"How do you know?"

"Mr. Jarvis told me. He saw the nest when he was mend-

100

ing the church clock. He says they nest there every year."
Sara paused, and Simon thought there was something
funny in her voice, as though she were holding something
back.

"Have you ever been up there?"

"No." Sarah turned away, back into the room. "Let's
shut the curtain. I'm cold."

"Wouldn't you like to have a pet owl? I've seen people
on the telly who had pet owls. Better than rabbits."

"Maybe."

"Why don't you ask Mr. Jarvis to let you see them?"

Simon was curious, but Sara was huddled back in bed
now, under her jumbled blankets and eiderdown. "Come
on in," she said. "Shut the curtain."

Simon came in. But he didn't stop talking. He never
gave up easily if he thought there was something to discover. "You're scared of them," he said. "I think you're
scared of the owls, too!" He was about to make a mock-
ing whoo-hoo noise, when another shriek, quite close outside the window, stopped him.

Sara looked angrily at him. "Well, they've been cursed,
that's why! They really are haunted, if you like!"

"What d'you mean?" But it took quite a lot of questions from Simon before Sara would say anything more.
She had meant to shut him up, and had forgotten how
annoyingly persistent he could be. At last she gave in,
and told him what she had learnt about the owls from
Mr. Jarvis. She knew she could not tell it as well as Mr.
Jarvis had told her, but she did her best. Simon lay in
his bed in the dark, and listened.

Mr. Jarvis was their neighbour, and an amateur his-
torian as well as a churchwarden, so he had a small collection of old books about the history of the village. One
day about a month ago, when he had been cutting the
grass in the graveyard, Sara had asked him about the big

old grave in the middle of the churchyard. He had told her it was the family grave of the Mowbray family. "They was always lords of the manor here until about ten years back," he had said. "So their grave has to be big, see, because they're all buried under it. All but one, any-road."

"All but one?" Sara had been curious.

"Yes. That one was Lady Mary Mowbray, who died in about 1580, or thereabouts. You can see her grave, if you look, over there in that bend in the wall."

Sara had been to look. The grave looked very small and lonely, compared with the impressive tomb that the rest of the family had. It was just a hummock overgrown with grass, with a small, worn headstone. She had asked Mr. Jarvis why it was apart from the rest. He had just been packing up his scythe to finish work, and he told her to come back to his house with him. Once there, he had washed his hands, made a cup of tea, and then hunted out an old book.

"She's buried over there by the wall," he had said, stabbing his finger on the table in the way he did when he wanted to make a point, "because she's not properly in the churchyard at all." And then he had sat back and taken a long swig of tea, leaving Sara to wonder politely what on earth he could mean.

But he could prove it, of course. Mr. Jarvis always could. He got out old maps of the churchyard which proved there had been no bend in the churchyard wall where Mary Mowbray's grave was until 50 years ago, a long time after she had been buried. All the time before that her grave had been in the field outside the church-yard.

"Why?" Mr. Jarvis had said. "You may well ask, young lady. Well now, look you here." And he had got out a dusty old history book, the sort he was always buying in second-hand bookshops, and fumbled through it until he had found the place he wanted. This is what he read.

" 'In 1576 Caroline, the favourite child of Mary, Lady Mowbray, was taken sick of a fever and died, aged only fifteen months. But when the child was buried, and the bishop attempted to console the mother, she flew out in a rage at him and his priests, cursing, and saying: "Wherefore should I any longer worship your God, when he permits the very owls to breed in the belfry without harm, and yet he could not save my daughter? I think I had rather be an owl, then, than a woman who kneels to your cruel God!" And from that day onwards, though the priests did what they could, she avoided them, and her husband, and all men. She never came again to the church, but wandered instead in the fields, talking to the birds, so that folk thought her mad or bewitched. And when the time came for her to be buried, the priest would not have her in the churchyard, for he said she was a heathen woman who had cursed the Lord.' "

"So then she was buried outside," Mr. Jarvis had gone on, "until 1920, when the vicar took pity on her and let her in, by making that bend in the wall that we saw. But 'tis my opinion, young lady, that that's not the end of the affair. I've thought about this here tale many a time, and it seems to me there's more to those owls than most are willing to admit. You may well call it superstition if you like, but I've lived here nigh on sixty years now, man and boy, and every summer I've thought there's something funny about those owls. You won't have noticed it, maybe."

"What things?" Sara had asked.

"Well, now there's that old yew tree that grows next to Mary Mowbray's grave, you'll remember, just over the path, and every spring you can see an owl sitting there, just after dark, before they goes hunting. Maybe nothing to it, but I asks myself why you don't never see them there any other time of the year. Then, every year, come midsummer, there'll be one or two little owls on the floor in the tower, in the bell-ringer's room, under where they nest. They don't look starved or nothing; they're just dead, as though they flew too soon or were abandoned, like. There's been years I've tried to climb up there and see if I could save them, but I never could. I wouldn't like to go up there this time of year. There's that screeching and flapping of feathers and claws at you, you'd think they was very devils. I broke my leg on the stairs once, trying to get away from them. I never seen no other owls so fierce—and frightening, too, somehow. I reckon,"— and here Mr. Jarvis had put his cup down and looked fiercely at Sarah, "—I reckon they're cursed somehow, even now. That woman's cursed them, and it's not such a curse as you can so easily remove. Whatever the vicar says."

Sara told all this to Simon as best she could, while they lay in bed, hot and sleepless on the summer night. She had a good memory, so she could tell him almost the exact words Mary Mowbray was supposed to have said. Very far away, they heard the last train rattling through the next village, an arrow of light in the darkness. Sara's father had stopped playing the piano for a while, but now a new groaning sound started up—the oboe. She thought it was a good story when she told it, so she was angry when Simon said, out of the darkness:

"Yeah, you don't believe all that, do you?"

"'Course I do. Mr. Jarvis knows what he's talking about. And anyway . . ."

"Yes, anyway?"

"There's something funny about the owls," said Sarah lamely. How could she explain the strange feeling she had had, more than once, when a great white bird had flown

104

silently past her in the dusk? Sometimes, she had had the feeling that they were hovering round her, following her—why her?

"Well, all owls seem funny to me. Anyway, how could she have cursed them? What would the curse make them *do*?"

"I don't know. I suppose it kills their chicks every year. I suppose that when they go near her grave, she curses them somehow, and their chicks die."

"But why should she want to do that? You said she wanted to *be* an owl, she didn't want to hurt them."

"Oh, I don't know," said Sara, puzzled. "But they're cursed somehow, I know that. I don't like it when they come near you. They look almost human sometimes, with those big eyes staring at you."

They lay silent for a while, both thinking about the owls. Sara was remembering the evening, a few days before Simon had come, when one of them had seemed to follow her all the way home, silently floating to and fro above her as she came past the churchyard in the dusk. And it had shrieked just as she had gone indoors. She wished they did go "whooo-ooo", like tawny owls. The shriek they made was so weird and searing—almost human.

Simon's voice broke in on her thoughts. "How would that old Mr. Jarvis get up to their nest, anyway? It's right up the church tower."

"Up the stairs, of course," said Sara. "There's a staircase in the tower. It's quite easy. I went up there last winter, but I never saw any owls. They probably hide in one of the rooms at the top, near the bells."

"I suppose they lock the church at night?"

"No," said Sarah. "I don't think so. The vicar says God's house is always open." Then she suddenly realised what Simon was thinking.

"I know what I'd like to do," said Simon. "I'd like to go up there, now, and have a look."

"Oh no! No, we couldn't!"

"Why, are you scared? They're only owls, you know, they can't hurt. I've got my torch. We could get out of the window, get across the road and be up on the tower in two minutes. We'd be back before anyone knew."

"But we can't go into the church . . ."

"Why not, if it's open? You're a coward, that's all, afraid of a few old birds! I *dare you*! There—if you don't take the dare, you're just a little scared baby, like all girls."

"It's not just the owls I'm scared of," said Sara, trying to get out of it. "It's something else . . ."

"There's nothing more. Just spooky stories. Come on, I'll be with you. We'll have the torch."

And somehow, Sara found that it was more important to take the dare than to be afraid. She would never have thought of this for herself, yet now that Simon had suggested it, she felt a little movement of gladness in her, as though part of her had always wanted to go. They dressed quickly, in dark clothes, and listened for a moment before they crept out of the window. The oboe was still groaning in the almost soundproof room. There was no sound outside but the rustling of wind in the trees, like a distant sea.

There was an easy way through the hedge at the bottom of the garden, and the churchyard was no distance away. They met no one on the road. Simon muffled his torch in a pullover, only flashing it briefly when he had to.

The moon was half-full, and the grey headstones gleamed over a grass that glistened silver in between the black shadows. They hesitated for a moment before crossing the open space between the lych-gate and the church, and as they did so, something flittered quickly past them.

106

"What was that?" said Simon, trying to flash the torch at it.

"A bat," said Sara. Another bat flittered by in its clever, jerky way. She thought Simon's voice sounded suddenly less confident than it had in the bedroom.

"I thought it was a black owl," he said.

Then, as they walked quietly along the path and round to the front of the church, the owls came. They came from nowhere, suddenly, two white birds floating back and forth over their heads, soundlessly. They were only a few feet away, and they could see the wings beating, but the owls made no sound at all.

"They're following us," said Simon. "Go on! Git! Shoo!" He waved his arms and flashed the torch at the birds, but they took no notice. For Sara, it was just like the other evening, and, just as then, she felt both frightened and happy. There was a tingling in her spine, and her head felt light and clear, as though a song was beginning in it.

They reached the church porch, Simon hurrying in front. Sara remembered how it looked in the day, with all the notices about Women's Institute and parish meetings on the boards. Now the notices were hidden in the gloom, and they had to flash the torch to find the brass handle on the great oak door. It turned with a great clank, and the door creaked open.

"Cor! What a noise!" said Simon. But his voice sounded small and uncertain as it echoed in the vast cave of the church. He flashed the torch uncertainly. Sara walked in. A pale light came through the arched stained-glass windows, and she could just make out the pews and the altar. She hummed a note to herself, under her breath, and for a moment she felt she could hear the same note sing in the walls of the church, as her father could make a glass sing by making a certain note on a violin.

"Which way?" said Simon, tugging at her arm hurriedly. She pointed to the back of the church, and he went there quickly, flashing the torch before him. She followed more slowly. Simon was a little scared, and hurrying to hide it; and for a moment Sara felt scared too, but almost immediately the other, glad feeling came back—the feeling that it did not matter what she felt, for something was happening that was too important to be frightened of.

They had to go through a screen at the back of the church, and then Sara pointed out the little wooden door in the wall that led to the tower steps. It was locked, but the long iron key hung on a hook beside it. Sara was getting it down when Simon gasped and yelled: "Oh no! Git out! Go on, git!"

She turned round. He was shining the torch on the back pew of the church; and on the pew, still and white in the torchlight, an owl sat and watched them. It had its back to them, but its head was turned right round on its shoulders. Its eyes shone red in the torchlight.

"Go on! Git! Shoo!" There was a scared sob in Simon's voice as he went desperately towards the owl, waving his arms and shouting. When he was a few yards away, the owl stretched its wings and flew, calm and silent, towards the church door.

"What's the matter? We came to see owls," said Sara.

"They shouldn't be in the church. They're not natural. They're following us," he said, his voice scared and not at all confident now.

"They know what to do. She has troubled them long enough," said Sara. She said it in a voice older, more mature than her own.

"What? *What did you say?*" Simon hissed, staring at her, the hairs tingling at the back of his scalp.

"I . . . I don't know," said Sara, in her normal voice. "It doesn't matter. Come on. I've opened the door." She had understood what she had said when she had said it. It didn't matter about explaining.

She led the way up the winding stairway. Simon had the torch, but it didn't matter. She could feel her way in the dark. Like an owl, she thought. They came to the first landing, a sort of empty room as wide as the tower. The bellringers' ropes hung from the ceiling in loops. Simon flashed his torch around.

"Is this it? Do they nest here?"

"No," said Sarah. "It's the next landing. In the corner of the small room to the left of the bells." She could see it in her mind as she spoke, though she had never been there.

"All right. Come on then," said Simon, making an effort, and pulling himself together. After all, it was his dare. There was really nothing to it. "I'll go first. Stupid old owls. They're only birds, anyway." He went over to the little door which led to the steps going upwards. Then it happened. He had opened the door and had put his first foot inside when there was a wild shriek and a hurricane of white feathers and claws flew out and struck him. The torch flew out of his hand and, as its beam flashed around the room, Sara saw Simon stumbling backwards with his arms thrown up to protect his head from the wild white beating wings of the two owls.

"Stop!" she said. "Stop!" And as the torch came to rest in the corner, showing a little patch of red light against the wall, she saw the two owls leave Simon and sit calmly on a windowsill, preening their feathers briefly and then looking at her. Simon sat on the floor, crying. She picked up the torch and looked at him. His cheek and arms were scratched, and his face was bruised and smudged with tears, but his eyes were all right.

Sara was quite unafraid now. Her head felt very light, and the clear singing note that seemed to echo everywhere, inside her and in the walls of the church, filled her with the knowledge that at this moment she was not only herself but someone greater than herself, and that she had something to do which would help someone who had been here much longer than she had, and who had to be set free. Something that was nothing to do with Simon. She looked at the owls, and as she walked towards the stairs, they flapped their soundless wings, and perched on her shoulders.

On the second landing, in the corner of the little room by the belfry, she found the baby owl. Its feathers were only half grown, and it staggered helplessly around on the floor, amongst old mouse and bird bones and a few owl pellets. The owl's nest, where the other chicks sat on a bigger heap of bones, was on a ledge several feet higher, by a little windowslit which opened on to the air. A few feet away from the chick on the floor was a drop which led down past the bells to the bellringers' room fifty feet below.

As she picked it up, Sara thought of the grave at the edge of the churchyard, and she seemed to see the face of the woman, Mary Mowbray, who had cursed God because she had lost her child. She seemed to hear her voice: "Wherefore should I any longer worship your God, when he permits the very owls to breed in the belfry without harm, and yet he could not save my daughter? I think I had rather be an owl, then, than a woman who kneels to your cruel God!" And Sara knew that Mary Mowbray had had to return every spring, and be an owl as she had asked, and suffer the death of her child again, until someone should come to rescue it and set her free.

And then the voice came again—a voice as distant as the clear singing in her head, and as close as the owls that perched on her shoulder: "Take the child. Care for her. I have been an owl long enough. Set me free."

Sara held the owlet and stroked it. Half-down, half-feathers. "I will," she said, though there was no one there to hear her. "I will care for it. Go free now." And as she turned to carry the young owl back down the stairs, one of the owls, perhaps the mother, left her shoulder and flew out through the little windowslit into the night air, where it flew in soundless circles round and round the church tower, higher and higher, not hunting, but rejoicing in its silent freedom.

THE MAN WITH THE BEARD

by ROSEMARY TIMPERLEY.

AFTER school one day, Alan went home with his friend Roger, the Doctor's son. They had tea in Roger's room, did a tiny bit of homework, then started a mock-quarrel which ended up as a wrestling-match on the floor. Mrs. Laycock, Roger's mother, came in.

"You boys! Every sound you make goes thundering through to the surgery. The patients will think we're a madhouse. If you want to fight, go into the garden and do it."

The boys obeyed, Alan sheepish, Roger irritated. "It's always the same," he grumbled. "I'm always having to keep quiet because of the patients. What shall we do?"

The garden was large and rather wild. It was home ground to Roger, so he saw nothing special about it, but to Alan, who lived in a block of flats, it was delightful.

"Hide-and-seek," he suggested.

"That's kids' stuff."

"It needn't be. I'll be a criminal on the run and you can be the fuzz."

111

"I'd rather be the criminal," said Roger.

"Toss for it."

They tossed a penny. Alan won the toss, so he was to hide and Roger to seek. His friend stood with his hands over his eyes and counted a hundred, and Alan ran at top speed to the far end of the garden, where there were trees and bushes. It was quite wild and wood-like down there, and as dusk was falling, mysterious shadows lurked among the leaves.

He found an old shed amid the greenery, opened the door and went inside. The place was cluttered up with junk, bits of furniture among the gardening implements, and there was a tall cupboard in the corner. This was empty, but for a few old jackets, so he got inside and closed the door. There was a handle on the inside, and he held on to that as he crouched in pitch blackness. He thought that if he held on to the handle and kept absolutely quiet and still, Roger, if he tried the door, would think the cupboard was locked.

It was only a game, yet suddenly he found that his heart was beating too fast, as if he really were afraid— really a criminal hiding from the Law. And when he heard Roger's footsteps crunching outside, he went as tense and sweaty as if it were the real thing. There was something sinister about this shed.

He heard the door creak open, then the clump of Roger's steps, the clatter of a falling garden tool, a curse from Roger as he stubbed his toe against something.

"You there, you villain? I'm the fuzz and I'm here to get you," said Roger.

Alan stayed silent and still. Now Roger was trying the cupboard door. Alan held on to the handle on his side. Then Roger apparently thought the door was locked and went away.

Alan heard the door of the shed close behind him,

then his retreating footsteps, and he was about to come out of the stuffy blackness of the cupboard, when he heard a sound in the shed—Roger must have crept back.

No. No, it wasn't Roger. It was someone puffing and wheezing and chuckling all at once. Someone quite old by the sound of him. Who could it be? Had a stranger wandered into the Doctor's garden—some down-and-out looking for a night's kip?

More chuckling and wheezing, drawing nearer, then whoever it was seized the handle of the cupboard door and tugged hard. Alan clung on to the handle on his side.

"Let go, you little devil," said a rough voice. "I know you're in there. I can smell you. I can always smell a nice little boy. You can't hide from me."

But Alan hung on like grim death. He wasn't going to let go—he wasn't—and he didn't let go. Instead, the handle came away in his hand, and the door swung open.

He shrank back against the wall of the cupboard as one of the most hideous faces he had ever seen peered in at him. It was dirty, thick-bearded, grey-skinned, with vicious little steely-grey eyes and an array of brown and yellow teeth grinning between pallid lips. A stench of decay filled the air.

"Get away from me," Alan gasped.

"Get away from you? You know I won't do that. You know who I am. Come on. Out of it."

"Very well, sir," Alan said politely. I must play it cunning he thought. He would step out calmly, then make a dive for the door of the shed. Being old, the man would be less agile than he—but he didn't think he'd have much chance in a hand-to-hand struggle. The other's hands were hard and huge, and he had monstrously thick shoulders.

Alan stepped out of the cupboard, putting an innocent expression on his face, then, quick as a flash, ran to the

113

door. He wrenched at the handle. The door didn't move. It was locked.

The man with the beard was chuckling.

Alan turned to face him. "Let me out of here," he said.

"I'll be carrying you out, in my own good time, when it's darker." He brought a knife from his pocket. Its blade glimmered in the dimness of the shed. "I'm not as handy with it as the boss," he said, "but good enough for what I have to do."

Alan's terror was so complete that he felt unnaturally calm. He's going to kill me, he thought. I'd better pray or something. "Our Father, Who art in heaven——" he muttered as the knife drew nearer and the hideous face came into enormous close-up—and then was blacked out as if an ebony shutter had closed over his eyes.

When he opened his eyes again, he was lying on the floor of the shed with Roger bending over him. "Keep still, Alan. Dad's just coming. What happened?"

Doctor Laycock hurried in.

"He was going to kill me with a knife. Where is he?" whispered Alan, but his voice was too faint to be heard by the others. The Doctor was examining his head.

"Nasty cut you've got there, Alan. You must have hit your head against that lawn-mower as you fell. Can you get up? Let me help you."

"You ain't half bleeding," said Roger.

Alan, helped to his feet by the Doctor, saw the pool of blood on the floor. "Is that mine?"

"It is," said Doctor Laycock cheerfully. "Head wounds always bleed a lot. Nothing to worry about. It's normal. Washes it clean, too. I'll give you a couple of stitches in the surgery and you'll be good as new. How did you manage to fall over?"

"I don't remember actually falling—it was the man——"

He brought a knife from his pocket . . .

"What man?"

"The man with the beard—a dreadful old man——"

"You've been dreaming while you were out for the count," said Roger. "There couldn't have been anyone in here. I guessed you were in that cupboard when I came looking for you, so when I left I locked the shed door, to give you a fright when you tried to get out. Then, when you didn't yell or anything, I came back to see what you were up to, and found you lying here."

"That locked door gave me a fright all right. You see——"

"Hold this pad lightly but firmly over the cut, like this," said Doctor Laycock. "Good. Now come along— and Roger——" He turned to his son. "Never, never lock anyone into a room or shed or anywhere else. Maybe you wouldn't care two hoots if it happened to you, but there is such a thing as claustrophobia. Did you panic a bit when you found you were locked in, Alan?"

"Anyone would have panicked, Doctor! You see, this man with the beard——"

But now Mrs. Laycock had arrived, all talk and fluster. "What on earth has been happening? Roger, you should look after your guest, not let him half-kill himself. What will his mother say?"

"Come on, Alan," said Doctor Laycock, and they retreated across the lawn, while Mrs. Laycock stayed to scold Roger, who was arguing that they were only playing criminals and fuzz and he hadn't done anything except lock the door of the shed—and how the hell was he to know that Alan was claustrowhatsit?

In the surgery, the Doctor gave Alan an injection in his forehead, so he'd feel no pain, then stitched up the wound, placed a pad over it, stuck it down with sticking-plaster, and tied a big white bandage round the lot.

"There! Now you look like a sultan," he said.

"You'd be a wow in the harem. Go along to the living-room, Alan. My wife will give you a couple of aspirins and look after you. I've still got some patients in the waiting-room and they won't go away until they've 'seen the Doctor'."

Grinning under his white turban, Alan went to the living-room where Mrs. Laycock gave him his aspirins and fussed over him kindly. Roger looked on with a touch of envy.

"I've telephoned your mother," she said. "You're staying for supper, then my husband will drive you safely home."

"It was that awful man—he might still be around——"

"What awful man, dear?"

"There's no man," Roger put in. "He had some sort of weird dream when he was knocked out."

"And it was your fault that he *was* knocked out, my lad," flared his mother. "Of all the stupid ways to carry on!"

"It wasn't Roger's fault. It was the man," Alan insisted.

"But no one could have got in!" said Roger.

Alan tried to clear his mind. Everything was muzzy still. There had certainly been no one in the shed when he entered, for the cupboard was the only hiding-place. After that, Roger locked the door. So—how *had* the man got in? But no dream could be as real as that—he hadn't been asleep—had he?

"Oh, my head aches!" he sighed.

But after a while the aspirins did their job and he felt better—even hungry. Also he rather fancied himself in his white turban. He'd wear it at school and everyone would be impressed and sympathetic—and he could make it an excuse not to do any homework for a week or so. Whacko!

Supper was delicious, and the conversation was interest-

117

ing. Doctor Laycock talked about his days as a medical student, rather gory jokes that appealed to Alan and Roger, especially a description of a battle in the dissecting-room, when the students divided into two camps and hurled corpses' innards at each other as ammunition.

"I remember I got a black eye from a flying gall bladder, and my best friend almost lost a tooth from a whizzing kidney," the Doctor said reminiscently. "Those were the days."

"How do teaching hospitals get bodies for students to practise on?" Alan asked.

"Some people kindly bequeath their bodies to medical science, in their wills, so they can go on helping the living after they're dead——"

"I've done that already," said Roger proudly.

"——and then," the Doctor continued, "sad to say, there are destitute people who die in the streets or in doss-houses or drown themselves—no known identity—no one to claim them—so permission is granted for their bodies to be used in the dissecting-room."

"Is there ever a shortage?" Alan asked.

"Do we have to discuss this sort of thing over our chocolate pudding?" Mrs. Laycock asked plaintively, but the three males ignored her.

"Sometimes, yes," said Doctor Laycock. "It's like anything else, sometimes a shortage, sometimes a glut. Of course, a century ago, in the early days of surgery, when surgeons were desperate to get hold of bodies to practise their skill on, there were the bodysnatchers to keep up the supply."

"Like Burke and Hare," said Roger, who had heard his father on this subject before.

"That's right. They stole bodies, or dug up graves to get them, and sold them to the hospitals or to private doctors. Then there was Bogg the Bodysnatcher—'the villainous

Nathaniel Bogg,' as the news-sheets called him. He used
to——"

"Darling, please!" his wife broke in. "I will not have
Nathaniel Bogg with my coffee!"

"All right, I'll stop," laughed the Doctor.

"Oh no—go *on*!" urged Alan.

"I have to tidy up the surgery after supper, so if you'd
care to come and lend a hand, I'll tell you then, before I
drive you home."

"That won't do his head any good," said Mrs. Laycock.

"It's made me forget I've got a head," said Alan. "If
you're interested in something, physical pains die down."

"That's what I often try to convey to my more neurotic
patients," said the Doctor, "only I daren't put it so bluntly
or they'd say: 'You don't believe I've got a pain!'"

Supper over, Mrs. Laycock commandeered Roger to
help her with the washing-up, as a penance for his "stupid
behaviour in locking poor little Alan in the shed", and
Alan followed the Doctor to his surgery.

"How is your head, really?" asked the other.

"Not too bad."

"I'll give you a couple of little pills so you'll get a
good night's sleep. Take a day off from school tomorrow,
and come here in the evening to have the dressing renewed.
O.K.?"

"Fine. Thanks. Now do go on about Bogg the Bodysnatcher."

"He's part of our local history, actually. One of the
houses at the end of this street used to belong to a nine-
teenth century medical practitioner called Doctor Carver
—most appropriate."

Alan chuckled.

"He specialised in children's ailments, had a good
119

reputation at first, then became obsessive about it and went round the bend. He needed a supply of children's bodies to work on in his private laboratory and hired Nathaniel Bogg to keep him supplied. But that wicked old villain didn't stop at grave-robbing. He took to kidnapping live children and cutting their throats."

As he talked he was tidying his desk, putting things in drawers or in the filing-cabinets.

"Doctor Carver and Bogg the Bodysnatcher, thick as thieves and partners in crime, carried on their gruesome trade for some years, but at last the Law caught up with them. There was a trial and they were both condemned to death. Have a chocolate—gift from a grateful patient."

Alan took a chocolate and sucked it. "Go on," he said.

"Carver the Cadaver, as he was nicknamed afterwards, was hanged by the neck until he was dead, as happened to murderers in those days, but Bogg escaped. He hid in the local wood."

"There isn't a local wood," said Alan.

"There was then, before this land was built on. The spot where this house stands was all woodland. If we could put back the clock, you and I would be in the middle of a woodland glade now instead of in this room."

The moon had risen outside and it cast strange shadows of trees on the walls, as the surgery was lit only by a small desk-lamp. Alan shivered.

Doctor Laycock continued: "The Law caught up with him at last, hiding in the wood. When he found he was surrounded, he cut his own throat with the knife he'd used on his victims. And they say——"

He closed the last of the crowded drawers and turned to Alan with a smile——

"They say that the ghost of Nathaniel Bogg still haunts these parts, and is still after the blood of any child reckless enough to wander alone—but you're all right, mate, because you'll be safe in the car with me—— Why, Alan, what is it?"

For Alan was standing petrified, cold shudders going up and down his spine.

"Oh, dear, have I been too blood-curdling for you? Roger loves these tales of gore and grue——"

"So do I, usually," Alan said quickly. "Tell me, what did he look like?"

"Who?"

"Nathaniel Bogg."

"If you'll hang on a second, I'll show you. There's an engraving made of him as he appeared at his trial—it's in this old book of local history——" He took a book from his shelf. "Yes, here we are. Ugly-looking customer, isn't he? Good thing that he's very dead."

"Yes," said Alan, as he stared in horrified fascination at the face of Bogg the Bodysnatcher. For it was the second time he'd seen that face this evening.

It was the hideous, evil face of—the man with the beard.

THE HAUNTERS

by MARY DANBY

EACH year, ten members of the Westhampton Boys' Club were invited to spend a weekend as the guests of Mr. and Mrs. Theodore Portly in their Georgian mansion. These visits to Blackwood Hall were enormously popular, not least because there were rumours that the Ancestors' Gallery, as it was known, was haunted.

Jack and Bill Simpson were among the visitors to

Blackwood Hall one year. Between them, they had a collection of thirty ghost books, and to see a real live ghost—or "a real dead ghost", as Jack put it—was their greatest ambition. Accordingly, Simpson and Simpson, Ghost Hunters Extraordinary, chose a moment after supper on the first day to corner Mr. Portly and ask him about the Ancestors' Gallery. They had already seen the gallery, and even by daylight it had looked strange and shadowy, its oak-panelled walls lined with Portly portraits dating back to the time the house was built. A fifteenth-century suit of armour stood to attention at one end, as though its first owner, Sir Cuthbert Portly, were still inside.

"Can't say I've seen any ghosts myself," said Mr. Portly, "but perhaps I'm not the ghost-seeing type."

He seemed more of a money-making type. The two seldom coincided, in the boys' experience.

"My wife, though," he continued, "she heard a bit of a whooshing noise once——"

"What sort of whooshing?" interrupted Bill. "Like wind, do you mean?"

"More like whooshing, she said." Mr. Portly held a match to his cigar. "Like somebody pretending to be a ghost."

"And was it, do you think?" Jack asked. "Someone pretending, that is?"

Mr. Portly sucked on the cigar, examined the end of it, and lit another match.

"What I think," he said slowly, "is that it's time I had a large whisky. Off you go, boys, and join the others. There's a nice game of ping-pong going on in the hall, by the sound of it."

Bill groaned, but Jack nudged him in the ribs. "Er, Mr. Portly," he called after the plump figure edging towards the drawing-room, "just one more question?"

Their host seemed to sag a little, but stopped politely. "Yes?"

"If there *is* a ghost, and it's a real one, have you any idea who it could have been?"

"Not the slightest," said Mr. Portly.

There was only one thing to do. That night, when the house was in darkness, the two boys left the bedroom they were sharing and made their way towards the Ancestors' Gallery. They slipped past the Portlys' bedroom, stifling their giggles at the sound of rumbling snores, and crept through the library, with its ceiling-high shelves of leather-bound books.

"Bet they've never even been read," whispered Bill. "Imagine having to wade your way through that lot."

"Ssh," replied Jack, opening the door at the other end.

The gallery was even more menacing by moonlight. The portraits seemed to stare and mock, as if sharing a private joke against the boys. Jack and Bill stayed close together, their shoulders touching, and waited.

"Perhaps it's not the ghost's night," suggested Jack. "Perhaps it——"

He stopped short as a noise came from one of the window-seats at the side of the gallery. "Ooo-ooo-ooo," it went.

"The ghost!" hissed Bill.

Then a white shape stepped from behind a curtain and slowly raised its arms.

"That's it," said Jack. "I'm off!"

They raced through the library, past the now-hiccuping snores and back to their bedroom. Bill collapsed on to his bed and sat on his hands to stop them shaking.

"Oh crikey, oh help, ooh-er," he kept saying.

But Jack was pacing up and down, punching his fists together and mumbling to himself. "It must be," he said.

123

"If that wasn't someone dressed up in a sheet and trying to scare us out of our wits, I'm a blue-nosed banana."

"Y-you're a w-what?" Bill's teeth were chattering.

"Look, it was one of the others. Dave, or Tony, or one of that lot. They overheard us planning our ghost-hunt and thought they'd have a laugh. Any fool could see it was someone wearing a sheet."

Bill had to admit he was right. After all, real ghosts are kind of filmy. They waft. They don't tread firmly out from behind curtains.

"Well then," Jack said. "We'd better see who has the last laugh."

The next day they were careful to make sure everyone knew their plans.

"We thought we might investigate the ghost tonight," Jack said casually. "Around midnight."

"In the gallery, you know," added Bill.

At five minutes to twelve, they left their bedroom, looking carefully around to see if any of the other doors were opening. Both were carrying sheets.

"We'll see who's afraid of ghosts now," said Jack as he opened the door to the gallery. "Quick. On with your sheet."

The two draped figures made their way to the nearest window-seat and each hid behind a curtain. They heard the clock in the hall below them strike twelve. Slowly, the door from the library opened.

"Now," whispered Jack.

Bill began making what he thought was a ghostly noise. "Ooo-woo," he went. "Whooooosh-woooo."

Jack peeped out from behind the curtain. Sure enough, another white-sheeted figure was advancing on them.

"Whooooo-er, boooooo," went Bill.

"Whoooosh," went the newcomer.

124

"Blast, we haven't scared him," muttered Jack. He moved out from the window-seat and stood with his arms raised in the middle of the gallery, trying to look spectral. The newcomer moved nearer, also raising its arms.

"O.K.," said Jack. "Who are you? Is it you, Tony?"

"Whooooooooo," said the newcomer, even louder.

Bill came out of his hiding place and stood beside Jack. "It's not fair," he said. "He's got a bigger sheet. Mine's so small you can see my pyjama legs."

"Shut up," said Jack fiercely.

"But it's only a joke," began Bill.

The newcomer was just a few feet from them now, and still advancing.

"Look, you can stop now." Jack's voice was beginning to tremble. "You've—you've had your fun."

It was Bill who screamed first. He realised, before it happened, that the thing in the sheet was going to walk right through him. Jack screamed when he felt the icy clamminess of nothing around him, turning his blood to water. Two hands clutched their hearts with fingers of cold menace, and the last thing they heard was a chuckling "whoooooooosh".

They stood with Peregrine, for that was the name of their new-found friend, at the library window, watching their funeral procession setting off for the church. It was gratifying to see how sad everyone looked.

"Did you watch your own funeral?" Bill asked Peregrine.

"Most certainly, old sport," replied the white sheet next to him. "It was most enjoyable. Of course, there were some who said I had been asking for trouble, dressing up like this to frighten Lady Blatherstone, but it was a fearfully good wheeze—even if I did trip on my sheet and impale myself on Sir Cuthbert's battle-axe."

"What do we do now?" said Jack.

Peregrine considered the situation. "For a start," he said, "I could give you some haunting lessons." He turned to Bill. "That 'Ooo-woo' of yours, for instance, was a little jerky. Try it after me. Ooooo-woooo. Like that. Nice and smooth."

"Ooooo-woooo."

"Better, old bean. Much better. Again, please."

The next year, six members of the boys' club team were thrown into quivering panic by the sight of three white-sheeted figures whooshing their way down the Ancestors' Gallery.

Back in one of the bedrooms, the boldest among them, Sam Coggins, said: "You needn't think a few boys in white sheets can scare me. No, sir. Come on, let's do a little haunting ourselves." He chuckled. "We'll see who has the last laugh."

Three echoes wafted past the door. A kind of chortling "whoosh", a groaning "aargh"—and a very smooth "oooo-woooo".

Armada Ghost Stories

Have you ever felt a ghostly "presence" in an empty room, or seen a shadowy figure standing by your bed?

Dip into one of Armada's hair-raising collection of ghostly happenings and feel those icy shivers run down your spine!

First Armada Book of True Ghost Stories

EDITED BY CHRISTINE BERNARD

Dare you enter the unknown world of spirits in these startling tales—all chillingly true? Read about the amazing Talking Mongoose, the despairing Man in the Iron Cage, and the dreadful curse on the Emperor's motor car. And study photographs of real ghosts!

Publication: December 1974.

Armada Ghost Books Nos. 1-6

EDITORS: CHRISTINE BERNARD AND MARY DANBY

Spine-chilling stories of spectres and hauntings by the score. Ghosts of all kinds—weird ones, wicked ones, frightening ones—even friendly ones! Collect them all—if you dare . . .

Armada

Armada books are chosen by children all over the world. They're designed to fit your pocket, and your pocket money too – why not build up your own Armada library? There are hundreds of exciting titles and favourite series to collect, and their bright spines look marvellous on any bookshelf. Armada have something for everyone:

Books by popular authors like **Enid Blyton – Malcolm Saville – Elinor Brent-Dyer – Alfred Hitchcock,** etc.

The best mysteries and most exciting adventure stories.

Favourite characters like **Jennings – William – Nancy Drew – The Hardy Boys – Biggles – The Three Investigators – The Lone Piners –** and many, many more.

Pony books by the Pullein-Thompson sisters, Mary Gervaise and Judith Berrisford.

A wonderful collection of famous children's stories.

Ghost books to make your hair stand on end!

A terrific collection of **quiz, puzzle and fun books** to entertain you for hours.

These are just a few of the good things Armada has in store for you.

If you'd like a complete up-to-date list of Armada books, send a stamped, addressed envelope to:

Armada Books,
14 St James's Place,
London SW1.

Armada